BRUTAL NIGHTS

A HIGH SCHOOL BULLY ROMANCE

HIDDEN VALLEY ELITE SERIES
BOOK FOUR

ISLA VAUGHN

ARROWSCOPE PRESS, LLC

Brutal Nights

Copyright © 2023 Isla Vaughn

(p) ISBN-13: 978-1-951919-47-4

(e) ISBN-13: 978-1-951919-46-7

Publisher: Arrowscope Press, LLC; www.arrowscopepress.com

Editing— Amanda K., Line Editor, Virge B., Proofreader, Rashida B., Beta Reader, Red Adept Editing

Cover Design—T.E. Black Designs; www.teblackdesigns.com

Interior Formatting & Design— Arrowscope Press, LLC; www.arrowscope-press.com

CHAPTER ONE

DAMON

#Busted

"Cheater!" Gia screamed when she and Skylar's mom opened the door.

Gia's shriek killed the post-orgasmic high from Sky's spectacular body as Sky straddled me on her too-small bed. The sensual glow radiating from her faded as she twisted on top of me to see who was in the doorway, then she screamed.

Sky's arms flailed as she frantically gathered her sheets and yelled, "It's not like that! It doesn't mean what you think it does."

My hands fell from her hips as she jumped off my dick. The look of horror on her face was a direct dagger to everything we'd just done.

"Skylar," her mom snapped, "your friend needs to go." Then she turned on her heel and left us with Gia, who stood with her hands on her hips, red-faced and glaring.

"I can't believe you did this to me," Gia accused, her big

brown eyes wild. Her hands went to her short blond hair and tugged. She looked unhinged.

I would have laughed, but Sky's reaction didn't sit well. *She still hates me.* Instead, I bunched one of Sky's blankets around me and casually leaned against the headboard, watching the show.

Gia needed to leave so I could get dressed and climb out the window, away from the shit show. Girl drama wasn't my thing, and the house was full of it.

With jerky movements, Sky yanked on her clothes. Gia whirled from the doorway, stomping down the hall. Sky threw a glare my way then ran after her. I had a bad feeling about the confrontation, so I got dressed, too, then followed.

The door across the hall from Sky's was shut. It had to be her mom's room. Only a bathroom and a little bit of hallway separated them. No wonder she'd wanted us to be quiet. I chuckled under my breath—she hadn't been. Not when she'd come apart in my arms. More than anything, I wanted to go back to that and skip the rejection she'd dealt me.

Heated voices led me to the family room, where I found Sky and Gia. And if looks could kill, both Sky and I would be dead.

"It didn't mean anything," Sky said, her voice strained and shaky.

Gia slapped Sky. The crack echoed through the room.

I wrapped my hand around Gia's wrist before she could do it again. "That's enough." I was angry. Gia was a bitch, and I didn't like her hurting Sky.

When she raised her other hand to hit me, I grabbed that wrist, too, before she could make contact. Then I pushed her away. She stumbled back, breathing heavily. The red staining her cheeks deepened, and her dark eyes glittered with hatred and betrayal.

Furious and disgusted with everything that'd happened, I strode to the front door. It killed me that Sky was upset, though I wasn't entirely sure why. It wasn't like I wanted more from her than her body and what she did to mine. I sure as fuck didn't care about her. *Right?*

Nothing about the current situation was good. And what I hated most, aside from the way Sky looked at me, was her denying what had happened between us, as if it meant nothing. It was my worst nightmare—*I don't want to be like my father.* The situation was too similar to what he'd done, and it made me physically ill.

Sky had glared at me one too many times after we'd gotten busted. *So fuck it.* I was out of there. That shit wasn't my scene. I yanked open the front door.

Sky caught it before it slammed behind me, and she followed me to my truck. Hand on the door handle, I paused as she crowded me, her hair wild from my hands, her lips swollen from my kisses. She was so goddammed beautiful, even when she was spitting mad.

"You used me." Her sensual voice cracked like the weapon she'd meant to yield it as, hitting her target like a heat-seeking missile. "You ruined my life, and now you're just going to leave so I have to pick up the pieces?"

The fuck? I hadn't left, but I sure as hell would after the way she'd rejected me. "This was a mutually beneficial thing between us. Don't pretend otherwise," I growled. "This is your problem. You're just some chick I don't give a shit about."

I got in my truck and headed home, knowing that what I'd said made me an asshole, but her dismissive comments had drawn just as much blood.

CHAPTER TWO

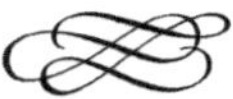

SKYLAR

#MyOwnFault

Everything was ten times worse. Gia wouldn't talk to me. My mom wouldn't stop talking to me, and Damon probably wouldn't ever talk to me again. Not that I cared.

Except I did.

Mom was waiting for me after Damon sped off and I went inside. Gia was gone—probably for the best. I ran my hands through my hair, the pressure of what had happened building to unbearable heights.

I shut the door behind me and leaned against it, reluctantly meeting Mom's eyes. I felt sick. Things couldn't have gone any worse.

"Sit," Mom said. "We need to have a refresher of 'the talk.'"

God help me. My face flamed with embarrassment, and I sat on one end of the couch while she took the other. I said nothing because what could I say? She'd caught me screwing Damon—while she was home. I was truly done for.

"I don't know what to address first." She ran her hands up and down her legs before clenching them into fists. "From everything that happened between Adam and me, I would have thought you would be more careful."

"What does Dad have to do with Damon?"

"Everything, since you didn't use a condom. And yeah, I saw that."

Oh... holy shit. I was in so much trouble. I assumed we had. In the heat of the moment, it didn't register that he hadn't used one. What a clusterfuck. I did a quick calculation in my head. I was supposed to get my period any day. I would be fine. *Right?*

I was far from okay. *What the hell will I do—about that, about Gia and Damon?*

"I don't want you to end up married because of one night. And what kind of boy is he? An athlete for sure with that body."

She did not go there. I dropped my face into my hands and groaned.

"And you let a boy come between you and Gia? While the potential pregnancy and being unsafe bothers me the most, that's a very close second."

"Mom—"

"No, Sky." Her expression closed off. There would be no convincing her of anything at this point. "You weren't being smart. By sleeping with that boy, you've risked your freedom, possibly compromised your health if he has an STD, and jeopardized your friendship with Gia. I'm not even going to address having him over and in your bedroom because I thought you were smarter than that. It seems we'll need rules."

Her phone rang, and when she glanced at the screen, a scowl appeared. She stood. "I have to answer this. But our discussion is not over. We'll revisit it tomorrow. Get some sleep. And no boys in the house."

Mom went to her room to take her call, and I went to mine. I fell onto the bed, which smelled like Damon. It made me both angry and sad. It only took one touch or kiss from him, and I folded. He had too much power over me, and I had no idea what to do about it.

I grabbed my phone and hit the button to call Gia. I wasn't surprised when she didn't answer, but a deep sense of panic and loneliness overwhelmed me, and I called her another eleven times. Then the tears came, and I was helpless to stop them. I cried so much that I passed out on my soaking wet pillow with my phone in my hand.

When my alarm blared from the too-close speaker, since I'd never set my phone on the nightstand, I peeled open eyelids as dry as the Sahara Desert. It took several tries to get any moisture in them. I cringed from the way my scratchy eyelids felt while I blinked a few times. Fuck that. I was sure I looked frightening.

It was Monday morning, and I was ditching school. I flipped onto my stomach after shutting off the obnoxious sound, then I checked to see if Gia had called or texted. My heart sank at the lack of notifications from her. But it wasn't like that for Damon. He'd texted several times.

I gave the screen a heartfelt fuck-you via my middle finger. He had no hold over me anymore, and I refused to answer. But I wanted to, and that made everything worse.

I tossed the phone on my bed then got up and washed my face, needing some coffee and toast. My head pounded, and my face was swollen and splotchy. When I got to the kitchen, Mom sat on the couch with a cup of coffee, staring out the window.

"Good morning," I said tentatively, my cheeks on fire and the weight of the world—or the potential topic of conversation—sitting heavily on my shoulders.

When she turned to me, I stopped, a coffee pod in hand, about to drop it into the machine.

Her eyes were dull, and her skin had an unnatural pallor. She didn't look like my vibrant mom. As she took a sip of her coffee, a tremor ran through her hand, and the tan liquid almost spilled. "Morning, Sky."

"Are you okay?" I left the coffee pod on the counter and went to sit next to her. Guilt tore through me. I'd done that to her. I was sure of it.

Mom patted my hand then stood. "I'm fine. Didn't sleep that well. That's all." A fleeting, half-hearted smile curved her lips. "I've got to get ready for work."

"Mom?"

She paused in the kitchen. Her barely touched coffee rattled in the sink as she set it down. "Yes?"

"I don't want to go to school today." I waved at my face.

Mom was a big believer in mental health days. I had straight As in school and a perfect GPA, so she didn't worry about me academically.

"Okay. I'll call you in, but no boys over."

"I know. I have a dinner shift that starts late afternoon. I'll go to that. Otherwise, I'll be home alone."

Mom came over and hugged me. "Okay, honey. I love you."

"Love you, too, Mom."

When she left to get dressed, I made my coffee and toast and took them back to my room. I spent the day reading and even watched an action movie. What I didn't do was think about how I'd lost my best friend.

By the time I arrived at work, my face wasn't puffy or blotchy like it'd been when I woke up. One good thing. Maybe the only one. Because when I started my shift, Gia and her new friends came in and sat in my section.

The restaurant was filling up, and after waiting on a lovely couple who were out for a date night, I approached Gia's table. Her hair was shiny and flattened, curving just under her chin. Her makeup was on point, and her clothes accentuated her abundant cleavage. She'd changed so much that I hardly recognized her as she laughed loudly with her fake-ass friends.

No point in introducing myself. They knew who I was. "Hi, everyone. What can I get you started with to drink?" I waited, pen poised over my notepad. I'd addressed Gia first.

The smirk curved her red lips before she even turned fully toward me. "I don't know what he saw in you other than a cheap fuck."

I pressed my lips together. That was what Damon would have thought of her from the barbeque she had made me go to over the summer, the one where she'd spilled a drink on Damon before falling to her knees to scrub his crotch. If I hadn't saved her, then and after, she wouldn't have experienced anything she'd dreamed of for her senior year. I wished I could go back and change that day. But I couldn't.

I couldn't do anything at the moment, and what I wanted to say to her would be in private.

Her brown eyes filled with hatred as she dropped her gaze to my chest. "No idea what he saw in you with that flat chest. But it was dark. Must've been a quick screw where anyone disposable would do." She tossed her menu at me. "I'll take a water and a side salad."

"Bring me a Diet Coke, and don't touch the straw." Rebecca grinned like I was the best form of entertainment. "Who knows how many diseases you might have after screwing half the guys in our class?"

Tina delivered another equally demeaning insult as she ordered. I barely kept my composure as I took their menus and left them to it. After putting in their meals, I grabbed Sarah's elbow and asked her if she would take my table. We swapped, and I got an elderly couple instead who had a ton of questions about the menu and ended up special ordering. Sarah wasn't the most patient, and I was overjoyed to help anyone who didn't attend our school, so it was a good trade.

I felt the glares from Gia's table the entire time they were there. Their food came, and I counted down the minutes before they would leave. When I thought they were close, I made sure I was in the kitchen. It was weak, but having my best friend belittle me and stand by while her fake friends did the same was more than I could handle.

When I went back on the floor, they'd left. The rest of my shift was uneventful and passed quickly. It wasn't until I went outside at the end of the night that the tears came again. My car was once again undrivable—last time, it wouldn't start. It currently sat in the parking lot where I'd left it, lopsided from two flat tires.

CHAPTER THREE

DAMON

#IDidntDoIt

I drove by the restaurant where Sky worked at the exact moment she came out. It was a coincidence, nothing more, and I pulled into the parking lot. As I parked next to her, she swiped angrily at her cheeks.

Is she crying?

Then I noticed her car had two flat tires. "Do you need a ride?"

She whirled around, her long hair swinging behind her in a midnight wave. I grinned as she stomped to the passenger side and yanked open the door before throwing herself inside. She was cute when she was angry. And to be honest, I was still upset over her comments from last night.

Arms crossed and eyes flashing fire, she snapped, "Perfect timing. But I'm sure you planned that when you tampered with my car. This way, I have to spend time with you."

I snorted as I reversed then drove out of the lot. "A shitload of girls would kill for me to bring them home. I don't need to tamper with anything."

"You're arrogant and full of yourself."

"Yet you're in my truck anyway." I sighed. We wouldn't get anywhere like that. "I didn't tamper with your car. And I wanted to give you a heads-up that while you weren't in school today, Gia and her new friends told everyone what happened." I wouldn't take the time for any other girl.

I didn't care about the girls I slept with—something I suspected I'd inherited from Dear Old Dad—and Gia was a front. I could easily squash her like a bug in front of the entire school. The only thing that held me back was how it would affect Sky. For some reason, Gia meant more to her than she should. I didn't see it. The girl had dropped her best friend and stabbed Sky in the back, who Gia didn't even know had gotten her everything she currently enjoyed.

"I already know." Her voice lacked some of the anger. "They were in the restaurant tonight and were particularly cruel."

"What the fuck did they say to you?" My hands tightened on the steering wheel. It didn't sit well with me. I wanted to do something to make it all go away for Sky.

"It's more like what they didn't say. It was stupid stuff. Innuendos that I was a slut. And they ripped on my flat chest."

I snorted. "You're hardly flat." Her breasts were perfect. "And if you were being compared to Gia, you've got nothing to worry about." Because Gia didn't do it for me. "You need to be prepared if something like that bothers you. The mean girls will eat you alive tomorrow."

I didn't touch the slut comment because it pissed me off. I knew firsthand she wasn't. Images of the first time we'd had sex played through my mind, and I had to adjust myself. I was hard from the moment she'd gotten in the truck, and it just got a hundred times worse.

"Yeah. Great advice from someone like you." She stared straight ahead, her fingers digging into her arms. "You'll be revered for being fought over by two girls."

"Do you want me to talk to Gia?" What I wanted to do was humiliate her.

"No. She's my friend. I need to handle it."

I wasn't so sure about that. "How can you call her a friend when she treats you badly?"

"I deserve it, and she can be mad about what I did. Besides, I won't fight back. She wants you, and I'm not standing in her way. But it sucks, and I hate it. I feel so alone," she whispered.

I pulled up to her house. "You aren't alone."

When she turned to look at me, tears glistened in her eyes. "I lost my best friend."

What can I say to that? I didn't think the girl deserved Sky. "I'll call you later."

"No. You don't need to." She slipped out of my SUV and hurried to her door.

I waited until she was safely inside before pulling away. Dark emotion swirled inside me. I didn't like that my hands were temporarily tied regarding Gia. She needed to be knocked down several pegs until she had to crawl back to Sky for forgiveness. Somehow, without making Sky mad, I would fix it.

CHAPTER FOUR

SKYLAR

#TeamGia

The sneers, whispers, pointing, and laughter made it clear when I walked into school Tuesday morning that I was the butt of everyone's joke, a new target to be ridiculed. Some shunned me as I went to my locker, head held high. Then there were the groups that stopped talking altogether when I walked by. Eyes followed my every move, and I hated it. Being under public scrutiny felt like hundreds of fire ants crawling over my skin, primed to bite.

The attention was foreign and very much undesired. I had kept a low profile before on purpose. I liked my privacy.

As quickly as possible, I found my locker and swirled the lock, inputting my combination until it popped open. The cool metal in my hand and my backpack halfway inside, I paused when I spotted a group of girls wearing shirts with #TeamGia printed across their chests.

What the hell is that about? And how did Gia get this popular?

Tucker fell against the locker next to mine, wearing a frown. "What's going on with everyone?"

I shrugged, unwilling to repeat last night's horror show. "If you haven't heard about what happened the other night, I'm sure you will."

Two girls walked by, giggling. One of them coughed "slut" into her hand, and my cheeks heated.

Fuck my life. Resting my forehead on my closed locker for a minute, I tried to calm down. Then I straightened, hugging my textbooks for first and second period to my chest like a shield—not that they would do any good.

"Are you all right?" Worry swam in his eyes as he took in my expression then bounced around the hall.

I shrugged. *What can I say?* "I'll survive."

He watched another couple of girls with the stupid shirts and shook his head. "Gia's been your best friend since, what, fourth grade?"

"Second." I had to work hard to build that shield back up. I didn't want anyone to see my emotions or that people's actions hurt me.

"What's going on here doesn't happen because of a friend."

He wasn't wrong—*but I owe her everything.* "She has a reason to be mad."

"If you say so." He pushed off the locker. "Come on. I'll walk you to class."

I fell into step beside Tucker, thankful to have at least one person in my corner. I held my head high as I walked through the halls to my first-period class. I had to see the day through without letting anyone witness me break.

"Thanks, Tucker. I'll see you around." I smiled, determined to look unaffected outwardly, regardless of how I felt inside.

"I'll be around, Sky." But his eyes weren't on me as he spoke. "Let me know if you need me for anything."

I followed to where he was glaring. Damon, Phoenix, and Shane walked down the hall, still several classrooms away, with about ten girls swarming around them. Somehow, Damon seemed to have become more popular, or at least no one was talking about him negatively or coughing "slut" as he passed. It wasn't as if I expected anything different, but one could hope.

And honestly, it was too much. I couldn't handle the sight of him and his cousins, so I went into the classroom. At my desk, I kept my head down or focused on the teacher, determined to block everything else out.

What made the class hardest was when Gia walked in a half second before the bell rang, a hot pink #TeamGia T-shirt stretched tight across her breasts. First hour was my only class with her. And luckily, she didn't have any of her cohorts there, and she left me alone. But even that hurt.

When class ended, I waited for everyone to leave before getting up myself. I had nothing to say to her—not publicly, anyway. Phone in hand as I walked out, I read an email from the administration office. My chemistry class had been switched back to second hour. Something about an error with the number of kids in the other class, and the approval should never have gone through in the first place.

Damon would be in that class. Not that I cared. It shouldn't be a problem. Not anymore. Gia was done with our friendship —aside from ridiculing me. And he could move on to whoever he wanted to sleep with next. Our arrangement was over.

A hard shove to my back took me by surprise, and my phone flew out of my hand. People laughed. Panic shot through me. Nerve endings tingled down my arms to my fingers as I dropped my books, trying to brace myself for the hard fall. But it never came.

Strong arms wrapped around me and hauled me against a hard body. I was shaken up. With trembling hands, I pushed my hair out of my face and looked at who held me, intending to thank them.

My eyes clashed with deep-blue ones, and my heart sped up. Anger pulled Damon's features tight as his gaze tore from mine, and he followed someone who passed by. I shifted my focus to see who it was.

Gia.

From the corner of my eye, I saw Phoenix bend and pick up my stuff, but he made no move to give it to me. Damon released me, his hand locked on my hip. I didn't move from his side. Gia slowed and looked me up and down.

"Slut."

"Knock it off," Damon growled. "Two weeks ago, you were nothing. Invisible."

Gia stilled, a deer caught in headlights. Phoenix chuckled then handed me my stuff. I took it, my body numb.

The air felt charged with menace, and I peeked at Damon's face. He looked like an avenging angel, disgust and cruelty evident in the sharp angles and planes of his features. His body shifted to shield me but intimidate Gia.

"Do you want everyone to know about your four-point plan?" he threatened.

From the way her face paled, she'd heard the warning loud and clear. And she now knew that Damon was familiar with the senior goals she'd confided in me before school started. It was a list she planned to achieve, one milestone for each quarter—get invited to the Ring, get a popular boyfriend, lose her V-card, and finally, become prom queen.

I sucked in a breath. "Stop." I shifted, no longer facing Gia but Damon. My palm to his chest, I pleaded, "Please."

I could tell he wanted to defend me, which wouldn't end well for Gia. What he could do would devastate her and end her coveted rise to prom queen. If I had to suffer through a few days of hell so she got her happily ever after, it wasn't that big of a price to pay.

My fingers fanned out, and I held his stormy gaze then whispered for his ears only, "I don't need a hero."

He tucked a few strands of my hair behind my ear, his mouth

softening as one corner quirked up. "Ah, but you do." His volume matched mine, as if we were in a temporary bubble. "For some reason I don't understand, you feel like you can't fight back. And the crazy part is, if anyone had done this to Gia, you would have annihilated them. What does she have over you to make your loyalty so absolute?"

I shivered at his astute analysis. "Everything," I whispered then turned and walked into chemistry.

The seat next to me was empty, and I wasn't sure if I would have my old lab partner back, but I refused to look toward the back of the class and check if she was there. The "slut" coughing continued, and people laughed. One guy asked if I was into reverse cowgirl.

Another, who I hadn't even known was in that class, leaned against the table.

When I looked up, he said, "I thought you were frigid. Guess I was wrong. You can ride me any day, baby."

That one I couldn't ignore. "Fuck off."

They were all a bunch of assholes. He laughed as he pushed off the table and went toward the back of the room. The bell rang just as a big body dropped into the seat beside me.

I didn't need to turn my head to know who it was. I could feel him. Every cell in my body was hyperaware of his presence, and a low hum of sexual tension buzzed between us, despite my misery.

"Hey."

His voice was soft, and I turned toward him, my eyes filling with tears.

"Are you okay?"

I wasn't. "I'm fine. Mind your own business."

But my voice cracked, and his mouth pressed into a hard line.

"Don't let them see you cry. They'll never stop if they know they're getting to you."

I sucked in a breath and released it slowly. I knew that. I just had to get through the day. And oddly enough, Damon sitting next to me, silently offering support, gave me the strength I needed.

After school, I would go to Gia's and explain everything. Things wouldn't ever be the same, but Gia had to know why I'd done it. *Most of it.*

CHAPTER FIVE

DAMON

#MrFixIt

The situation was bullshit. I broke off from Phoenix and Shane, who headed to practice, and went to find Sky at her locker. As far as I knew, her car was still in the restaurant's parking lot. As I turned down the hallway, I took in the scene. Her dark hair fell down her back in beachy waves, and her jeans hugged her ass and legs, making them impossible not to notice.

I wasn't the only one. A need to possess, to claim her as mine, roared through me when too many guys fixated on her as they filtered through the hallway. I closed the distance between us and fell against the locker next to hers, growing hard and ready instantly.

If Sky was sexy from the back, she was stunning and alluring from the front. A rare beauty both inside and out. And I wanted her more than I ever thought I would. *But haven't I always?* I was obsessed with the one girl who wanted nothing to do with me at school.

She finished stuffing her backpack with books, slung the strap over her shoulder, then shut her locker before facing me.

I hated saying it, but since she'd tied my hands—for the time being—it was the best advice I could give. "Leave Gia alone."

Her eyes darkened, and I already anticipated what she would say.

"For now," I stipulated. "Nothing you say to her can make matters right."

"I have to. She needs to understand why."

"It won't go well. She's too full of herself." Something I could easily change. And I would, when it wouldn't backfire and make Sky shut me out of her life for good. I told myself it was because I still wanted in her pants. I did, but there was more to it.

"Can you give me a ride home?"

She looked defeated, and I was defenseless against her silent plea for help. It would cost me. I had practice and would probably get benched, but it was the least I could do. "Sure. Let's go."

I glared at everyone we passed to get to my car. If anyone said anything to her, under their breath or otherwise, they would have hell to pay. At my SUV, I opened the door for her. The ride to her house was in silence, and I hated it, but unless she gave me free rein on Gia, things would be difficult for her.

I pulled into her driveway, and she paused before getting out. When her blue eyes met mine, my gut tightened.

"Do you want to come in?"

"Yes." More than anything.

We went into her house, and she dropped her bag near the door. It was a small house, and we'd walked into her family room as soon as we stepped inside. A strip of hooks lined the wall to the right in the four-by-four entryway, where a few light coats hung. Santa Monica weather never required anything too heavy. A decent-sized TV took up the wall closest to the front door. A worn dark-blue couch sat opposite it.

That part of the house was open concept, the kitchen separated by a peninsula with two barstools. I knew from prior visits that the hallway situated between the living room and kitchen led straight to a bathroom in a T-formation, with Sky's and her mom's bedrooms on either side. Her mom must not be home because it was quiet inside.

I sat on the couch next to her, letting her take the lead. I wanted to know if she was okay, but I sensed she needed a break.

"What do you do other than football?" she blurted then shifted nervously.

"Meaning? Hobbies?" I could do that.

"Yeah." She ran her fingers through her hair, pushing it back over her shoulders. "Do you have any, other than football? Favorite authors, that sort of thing."

I shrugged. "I don't have a lot of time to read for fun. This year, I stacked my schedule with several college-level classes, and between that and practice, I spend my free time with my cousins."

"That must be nice, to have built-in friends who are family. You've always seemed tight with Phoenix and Shane." She mashed her lips together. "That's sort of how Gia and I were."

I let go of the tiny window to discuss Gia. She still seemed on edge, and I wanted to wait until she was more relaxed to dive into that bullshit—and the other. I'd bought a pregnancy test for her last night. I wasn't sure how she would react, but I didn't want her to feel alone.

"They're more like brothers than cousins. Cole and I grew up with them. We always played ball together, which helped, as our home lives were fucked. Well"—I grimaced—"you know what happened with my mom. It's not a secret. And Phoenix and Shane's dad is a piece of shit. Being around my cousins… They make things easier to deal with at home."

"Have you all been accepted to Thane yet?"

"Yeah, pretty much. The coach reached out to each of us already. A verbal acceptance has been made, but signing day isn't until the winter. What about you? Where are you going?"

"I don't know. I have an acceptance letter from Thane as well as a scholarship package, which makes going there an easy decision. But some variables are up in the air, and I'm holding off on committing until I know everything's good."

"What variables?" *Does she mean the possible pregnancy?* I couldn't believe I'd forgotten a condom.

She shrugged. "I don't want to talk about that. But we do need to address our lack of condom the other day." Her fingers twisted together.

"Fuck, yeah, we do. That was bad. I can't believe I did that. I've never done that before. You just make me lose my head." She consumed my thoughts to the point that all logic went out the window.

She scowled. "Are you saying it was my fault?"

I grimaced. "Not what I meant. Stop being defensive."

She was scared, and if I thought too long about it, I would be too.

"I'm clean. I've never been with anyone else without a condom. Are you on the pill?"

"No."

"Are you worried? I bought you a pregnancy test. I thought we could do it together so you're not dealing with it alone." Christ, I couldn't even think of going down that path.

If she got pregnant, everything would change. *But would it be so bad, aside from how young we are?* I would prefer—as I was sure she would, too—that we get through college and establish careers first. But I was taking things too far. We weren't even in a relationship. So a kid wasn't really in the equation.

"I don't think there's a huge risk. But thanks. I'll take it in a few days, but the timing might've worked in our favor."

"Okay. I'm here for you, so don't shut me out. If you need anything—when you take the test, or whatever—I'm a part of this." I unzipped my backpack and handed her the pink-and-white box.

She set it on the end table by the couch. "Thanks." Her voice was soft, then her gaze dropped to my mouth.

I lightly wrapped my hand around her wrist and tugged her closer, more than okay with taking things in another direction. The topic had been a heavy one.

When she moved close, I lifted her hips so she straddled my lap then buried my hands in her silky hair. "I've wanted to do this every time I saw you today."

Her eyes dilated, black eclipsing the deep blue. Need for her exploded inside me, and I took her mouth in a punishing kiss. She wrapped her arms around me, her fingers anchoring in the hair at my nape. She kissed me with equal passion.

I explored her mouth as desire built until she squirmed on top of me, making my dick want to punch through my zipper to get inside her. I slid my fingers beneath her shirt and eased it up.

She jerked back. Face flushed and eyes sparkling with banked need, she shook her head. "Not here." She climbed off me, a seductive smile curving her swollen lips. She grabbed the test.

I followed her to her room, shutting the door and flipping the lock behind me—something we should've done last time to avoid all the drama. She tossed the test onto her desk as I pulled off my shirt. Her eyes flared with renewed heat.

Then I advanced on her. She shivered as my hands found her hips, easing the hem of her shirt up and over her head. I wanted to explore every inch of her. Her hands skimmed my chest, tracing my abs as she worked her way higher. The air felt charged, and I tried to go slow as I ran the pad of my thumb over her bottom lip then dipped it into the warm heat of her mouth. She nipped my finger then sucked it in, swirling her tongue around it, and I lost it.

I was on her like a man with his first drink after being stuck in the desert for three days. She was so sweet. I couldn't get enough of her. Her tongue teased mine, stoking the fire to a raging roar. Too many clothes stood between us. I popped the button of her jeans, undid the zipper, and shoved them down.

We had to break the kiss, breathing heavily and never taking our eyes off each other as we both tore at our clothes to get out of them quickly. I gazed hungrily at her as I guided her to the bed. With her head on the pillow, I spread her legs and traced my finger over her slick seam. The unbidden moan that tumbled from her lips told me she was more than ready for me.

That time, I grabbed a condom. And when I pushed inside her, I groaned at how right it felt. A haze of desire fogged my mind as we moved together. Every touch, kiss, and caress heightened our need until we found release in each other's arms.

After disposing of the condom, I held her, more content than I'd ever thought possible. We talked quietly until she told me I needed to leave before her mom came home.

I pulled out of the driveway and circled the block, parking in front of another house, then I walked to Gia's, not wanting to alert Sky's mom to my presence.

I rang the doorbell, and Gia opened the door with a big smile. I wanted to wipe it the hell away. Behind her, Tina and Rebecca, two sophomore cheerleaders who ate lunch at our table with Jessica, sat on the couch munching chips.

Gia's house was a close replica of Sky's in terms of how it was set up. The only difference was that it was a tad larger with a lot more clutter and filled with the mouthwatering scent of whatever her mom had cooked.

Gia reached to pull me inside, but I brushed her hand away and bypassed her. The other girls said hi, but I ignored them. When she followed me into her living room, I narrowed my eyes at her.

"We need to talk." Nothing about my tone or body language was friendly, and she should have been nervous. I studied her wide grin and relaxed posture. She wasn't. The false sense of security from her brief popularity must've filled her head and blocked my signals.

"Tina and Rebecca are good friends. Anything you need to say to me, you can say in front of them."

I snorted. *Idiot.* A calculated grin curved my mouth. I would enjoy the little dose of reality I was about to give her. And if Sky's feelings didn't matter to me, it would have been so much more fun. "They're not your friends. Skylar is, and if you want her to remain one, you had better stop being such a bitch to her."

Gia blushed, and I caught the quick side-eye she shot the other girls. "If Sky were my friend, then she never would have slept with my boyfriend."

"That doesn't matter. You need to think about what we were —or weren't." I went to the door, and with my hand on the knob, I delivered a small warning, one I hoped she would heed, for Sky's sake. "And if you don't leave Sky alone, you'll end up right back where you were. A nobody." On the other hand, I looked forward to her being an idiot. I wanted to go open season on her.

The door shut behind me with an ominous click.

Back in my SUV, I headed home and picked up the air compressor to take care of Sky's flat tires. It didn't take long to fix the problem, since her tires hadn't been slashed. The air had been released by jamming something into the air valve.

It wasn't something I would do for just any girl, but Sky was different. She'd gotten past my walls and under my skin in the best possible way. And I wanted to see her again. When I was done, I texted that I would pick her up to get her car.

CHAPTER SIX

SKYLAR

#CloseCall

Twice, Damon had come to my rescue after car problems. And in the back corner of my mind, I recognized he wasn't the one to cause them, which I'd accused him of in the first place.

I buried my face in my hands, mortified at how quick I had been to blame him. It was my go-to reaction for a guy I'd always viewed as an asshole. He could be but not always and not to me lately. His willingness to help me, to fix my car and rescue me, said everything. And even if I didn't quite verbalize it, he seemed to understand everything I was thinking. Because when I thanked him for helping me, I meant it.

I never thought I would feel like he was someone I could count on, but I almost did. I wasn't fully there because he was an athlete, and I hated them on principle. And even though things between Gia and me and at school were a nightmare, I had a reason to smile.

Music blaring, I pulled into my driveway and shut off my car. When I got out, I paused as a car stopped on the curb across the street not far from a streetlamp. It idled there, no one getting out, as if they were watching me. It was dark outside, and I squinted. I didn't recognize the car, but I was tired of people messing with me, so I planned to tell them to fuck off. Balling my hands into fists, I stormed over. But as I stepped off the curb, they slammed on the gas and pulled away. A chill raced up my spine as the car disappeared around the corner.

What the hell? Goose bumps raced over my skin, and I cast a wary glance up and down the street before hurrying inside. After I unlocked the door, I pushed inside then slammed and locked it shut behind me.

Mom paced the small length of our family room. Something was very wrong.

"Mom."

Her frantic eyes met mine, and she stopped a few feet from me.

"A car out front seemed like it was watching our house." I wrapped my arms around my waist. "There were no lights on, and when I went to investigate, the car sped away. It was really weird."

What I'd said fell on deaf ears. "The car doesn't matter." She dismissed what had unsettled me. "Creepy or not, we have bigger problems."

"We do?" I held still, waiting for whatever bomb she would drop.

Mom took my hands and led me to the couch. We sat, and her grip tightened.

"I got a call from the Department of Corrections." A tremor ran through her voice. "Your dad is due to be released sooner than expected."

Tears welled in Mom's eyes then spilled over and rolled down her cheeks. Her hands shook with fear, and I squeezed them, determined to be strong for both of us. I didn't remember much about him other than that he hurt Mom, which was a big deal. He gave me the scar on my temple—or I'd been told he'd caused it. I didn't remember when it'd happened, only the part where I'd hidden in Gia's treehouse until she'd found me. And then her family had saved us.

But deep inside me, fear of the man had festered, and I feared what that meant. What I might remember was hidden deep in my subconscious. The idea of him finding us and what he might do when he was out of prison terrified me.

"I don't want you to worry. We'll be okay. I just need to process this, and I wanted you to know what was going on too."

I hugged Mom, and we clung to each other for a few minutes until she pulled away. "I was going to make some dinner after I make another call."

"Sure." I stood and grabbed my backpack. "I'm going to get some homework done."

On my bed, I pulled out the books I needed for homework and got to work on them, but concentrating proved difficult. I wanted to call Gia and talk to her about what was happening. She would understand, but that option wasn't available to me anymore. *Because she hates me.*

An hour passed, and I completed my homework then had a tense dinner with Mom, where we were both on edge. When we finished, I cleaned up, and she got lost in a movie, which normally I would have watched with her, but I decided to read awhile instead.

I couldn't get the car out of my mind and stood inside my room, trying to convince myself it was probably someone who'd gotten lost. It wasn't a big deal. A thump sounded at my window, and I jumped, falling against the bed.

My heart raced as I went to peek behind the curtain. When Damon's face appeared, I sagged against the wall then unlocked and slid up the pane. He ducked and slipped a leg inside, but his head caught on the window.

"Oh, shit," he muttered as he stumbled into my room.

I curled my fingers around his arm, trying to stabilize him, but he was too heavy, and he took me with him as he hopped, twisted, then collapsed onto the bed. He fell on his back, and I lay sprawled across his chest. The lilac bedspread beneath him should have looked too feminine, but it only accentuated his masculinity. I liked him in my room, among my things.

Damon's carefree grin made me laugh. I tucked my head against his neck, enjoying the feel of his arms around me and the sound of his quiet chuckle. His arms tightened when I lifted my head and went to get up. Then his lips were on mine. His kiss was soft and sweet, with a tenderness that brought tears to my eyes.

He pulled back, concern creasing his forehead. "What's wrong?"

With a sigh, I rolled off him and sat on the bed, waiting until he got situated too. Then I told him about the car and my uneasy feeling about it.

"What kind of car was it?"

I bit my lower lip, relieved that he didn't dismiss me or tell me I was crazy, but I honestly didn't know the answer to his question, so I shrugged.

"Don't go near it again."

That dangerous box where I kept things locked away deep inside creaked open a hair, and I shivered. My hands balled into fists, and I barely felt my nails cut half-moons into my palms. The need to run and hide washed over me in an uncontrollable wave.

"Hey." Damon's deep voice persuaded me to focus on him as he gently pried open my hands. "It'll be okay."

I blinked then froze as I heard Mom's door open. It was directly across from mine. I shoved Damon, and he leaped off my bed, flattening himself against the wall opposite me. The door opened, obscuring him from view behind it. I grabbed my phone from the nightstand.

Mom stood in the open doorway, facing the end of my bed. A frown marred her face. "Who were you talking to?"

My pulse hammered against my skin, but I waved my phone with the back facing her. "I was talking to Damon on speakerphone."

"Okay." Her gaze skimmed the room, and her frown deepened as she crossed to the window.

I tensed. *Shit.* The door had blocked him from view as it opened, but Damon was so big she might see him when she turned to leave. In a quick movement, she yanked the curtain shut, and I jumped.

"You need to keep these closed now. We have to be careful and maintain good habits."

"Yeah, okay." I held up my phone again, making sure I kept my gaze on her and not where he hid. "I'm still on, so…"

She smiled, the tension in her face easing for the first time since I'd come home and found her pacing in the family room.

"Good night, Sky. I have an early appointment tomorrow, so I'm going to crash."

"Okay, night, Mom."

The door shut behind me, and I sagged against my headboard then laughed. Damon grinned as he left his hiding spot and stalked toward me, all devilishly handsome. It felt good to laugh, and it was all because of him.

When he sat next to me, I scooted closer and wound my arms around his neck. Before then, it had always been him who had initiated contact between us, but I wanted to be the one to kiss him.

CHAPTER SEVEN

DAMON

#Benched

Coach's punishment for ditching practice Tuesday was to run endless drills in the afternoon. When practice was over, I slammed into the locker room in a shitty mood.

Then Phoenix was in my face, his silver eyes a murky storm of anger. "What the fuck were you doing missing practice for that girl? Nothing is more important right now."

"Get off my back."

I shoved Phoenix, and Shane jumped between us.

"A lot of things are more important, and Sky's one of them," I said.

"You're missing the point." Phoenix reached around Shane and shoved me back. "You're not the only one affected when you do shit like what you did yesterday. If Coach benches you for the game this weekend, the team suffers."

Shane pushed us both back as I launched my fist at Phoenix. The punch went nowhere.

"Save it for the Ring," Shane growled.

I stormed out, hesitating a step as Phoenix's voice carried

over the background of slamming locker doors and running water.

"It's not just your future you affect."

His last comment hit me like a ton of bricks. He was right. I was being an asshole, but Sky needed me. My palms crashed against the door, and it swung wide as I exited the locker room. I didn't even know where to go with that thought, but it circled in my mind. It was uncharacteristic of me to put a girl before football and something to ponder for sure.

Gia's behavior wasn't my problem, and neither was how it affected Sky, but it got to me. She'd gotten to me. And she'd never wanted me until her tuba-toting band best friend, Gia, had wanted the impossible. Gia's four-point plan—to be a part of the Elite, to skyrocket her nonexistent popularity, to become prom queen, and to lose her virginity. It was Sky's loyalty that had brought her before me, after Gia had fucked it up. I couldn't believe my luck when Sky had approached me with a proposition to help her best friend, and I'd countered her offer with sexual favors from her instead, since I wouldn't get any action while pretending to be with Gia.

With Sky deeply ingrained in my thoughts, I drove by Chicks-N-Wings to see if she was there. It was packed with the dinner crowd, but her car wasn't in the parking lot.

She hadn't gone to school either. I pulled over and sent her a text. When it went unanswered, I tried calling but was sent to voicemail. I didn't like it. Something felt off. In the back of my mind, the suspicious car lurked, and I pulled a U-turn and sped toward her house.

No cars were parked on the curb around her house, but when I pulled into the driveway, the word "slut" was spray-painted on the garage door. I saw red, and it wasn't just from the color of the paint. That shit had to stop. The easy solution would be to call Gia out in school for her prior nobody status and how fake she had become, which would work if I didn't care about how it affected Sky. But my actions would, and Sky had made that clear. Having my hands tied because I *cared* sucked. I would have to devise another way, since she was so protective of Gia, even though the girl didn't deserve Sky.

I did the only thing I could at the moment—go to the hardware store for a can of primer and white paint. When I returned, nothing in the neighborhood had changed. I got to work on the door, doing a second coat after the first to ensure the red didn't bleed through when everything dried. And as I did that, I had an idea about how to manage the situation. One that wouldn't cause Sky to fly off the handle in protest.

As I closed the can of white paint, Sky's mom came out the back door.

"Thank you for doing that." She waved toward the garage door. "It… was bothersome."

Clearly, to both her and Sky, especially since they knew who did it. I couldn't help but wonder if Gia's parents had been made aware of the situation. By the pained look on Sky's mom's face, I somehow doubted it.

I nodded. I was partially the cause, since I'd let Gia hang around me as much as I had. She'd gained power. It wouldn't last, but some people saw her as an underdog, and that was what they supported. That and the chance to get close to my cousins and me by associating with her. Complete bullshit. Gia was spineless and insipid. The only reason I'd put up with her was to get closer to Sky, the one girl at the school who wanted nothing to do with me. And I really didn't want to go back to that, which was why I respected her choice in dealing with Gia.

"Come on in." Sky's mom held open the screen door.

"Thanks."

She looked so much like Sky, just older, and her eyes had a world-weary wariness that made my guard go up. Something was bothering her, and I doubted it was the spiteful graffiti.

"Sky's in her room. You can go in there, but leave the door open."

She held my gaze, and I nodded before she went back to the couch where she'd been watching a movie.

I went down the narrow hallway and turned right into Sky's room. The curtains were closed, but enough light filtered through to show a small lump under the covers. Leaving the door open, as her mom had said, I went in and sat on her bed. Sky lay on her side, curled into a ball, facing away from me. Her long, dark hair fanned across her pillow, a stark contrast to the white-and-lilac-colored pillowcase.

In sleep, she appeared innocent and peaceful. I brushed a few strands of hair off her cheek, quietly saying her name then jostling her shoulder slightly.

Sleepy eyes blinked me into focus, and her brows furrowed in confusion. "How did you get in here?"

"Your mom."

She sat up, scraping her hair back from her face, and the confusion cleared when she noted the open door. "What are you doing here?"

We needed to discuss two things. I went with the most life-altering one first. The TV was on, and I thought we would be okay, but just to be sure, I kept my voice low so as not to alert her mom.

"Did you take the pregnancy test yet?" I shoved my hands in my pockets, unsure of how Sky would react. I needed to know, though.

Wide blue eyes met mine, and she slowly shook her head. "I haven't gotten up the nerve."

"We should do it together."

A small smile flitted across her mouth, gone in the blink of an eye. "Are you going to pee on the stick for me?"

"If it worked that way, sure. Where did you put it?"

She pointed at the top drawer of her dresser.

I rested my hand on the handle. "May I?"

"Yeah." She pulled her knees to her chest and wrapped her arms around them.

I opened the drawer and moved some clothes until I found the pink-and-white box. When I pulled it out, I opened it and withdrew the directions. "One line is negative. Two is pregnant." I held the stick out to her. "Let's do this thing. Pee on the end, and after three minutes, we'll have an answer."

She pushed out a breath, flung the covers back, then dropped her legs over her bed and stood. Her hand curled around the test and pulled it free as she passed by me on her way to the bathroom. The door shut behind her, and I leaned against her dresser, waiting for her to come out. The toilet flushed, the water ran in the sink, and she was out. She placed the stick next to me on the dresser then returned to her place on the bed.

I set a timer on my phone then studied her. Her cheeks flushed pink, and her full lips turned down in a pout that, if I didn't know what had caused the look, would have been cute. I hated that I'd put us in our position, all because I couldn't resist her, and I'd lost my goddammed mind that first time we had sex.

"You know you're not alone, right?" I had to say it out loud. If she was pregnant, we would face that and whatever decision she made. I would stand by her.

"Yeah. Thanks." She spoke softly and kept her eyes downcast.

When the timer went off, she looked up in horror. "I can't do it." She shook her head, not moving an inch off the bed. Tears filled her eyes, and her hands shook before she clasped them around her legs.

I was just as freaked out as she was, but I wasn't the one who would face the changes she would go through if she was pregnant—or face the decision to terminate and how that might haunt her later if she decided to go that route.

I did what I could to shoulder as much of her pressure as possible, picking up the pink-and-white stick to check the control panel window. My knees went weak, and I would have fallen from sheer relief if I hadn't locked every muscle in my legs.

"Well?"

I grinned at her then flipped the stick so she could read it. "One line. Not pregnant."

The smile that curved her face was filled with relief, and her shoulders dropped almost an inch.

"I have an idea."

Her gaze was steady, almost trusting. "Okay, what is it?"

"People are pissed off at you because they think you stole me from Gia just for the fun of it."

She scowled, and I lifted my finger, slightly shocked at what I was about to suggest.

"But if they think you're my girlfriend, they'll ignore Gia's bullshit and move on."

An amused smile pulled her lips wide. "Are you asking me to be your girlfriend?"

It sounded crazy, even to me. I wasn't a romantic guy, and to make it believable, I would have to be. It wasn't real, but it felt like it was. "Until this blows over, I'm asking you to be my girlfriend." That was something I'd never had before.

Silence. Her blue eyes bore into mine, and I thought I saw a flicker of something, but it was hard to tell what. *Amusement? Does she think this is funny?* My hands curled into fists at my sides. There wasn't anyone else that I would even consider offering this to, and she had nothing to say?

It pissed me off, so I got up and headed toward her door. "Forget it. And have fun cleaning spray paint off your garage when it happens again."

I was at the door when she finally spoke.

"Wait."

CHAPTER EIGHT

SKYLAR

\#BFProblems

I *can ditch again.* My backpack was on, and I clung to the strap, contemplating tossing it to the ground and returning to my bedroom to hide from the bullshit at school. I hesitated, then Damon's black Range Rover turned into the driveway. My stomach was a mess of nerves, and if he hadn't pulled up, I would have chickened out.

But I'm stronger than that. For two days, I'd hid in my house and licked my wounds. It was time to get out there and strike back, or at the very least, stand my ground.

I needed to pull my head out of the sand and deal with everything. After squaring my shoulders, I left the house, locking the door behind me, since Mom was asleep inside. Then I went to the passenger door of Damon's SUV. That would be the start of our fake dating experience.

He turned the music down when I got inside then backed onto the street. He smelled so good I had to force myself not to move closer. The interior of the SUV was dark and clean, and while it was spacious, I felt confined by the way his presence took up so much of the space.

"We need to establish rules."

I turned to face him, already aggravated. "You're kidding, right?" *Could he be more controlling?*

Blue eyes framed in dark lashes that most girls would kill to have met mine. "I'm not kidding, so pay attention." He turned back to the road. "Rule number one. Don't be too clingy, but don't be indifferent either."

"Oh, so read your mind to know the exact balance? Sure, I'm on it."

"No PDA unless I initiate it. Not because no one will believe I did a one-eighty—"

"Because you're kind of a man whore, and it's in your nature?" I snapped.

He snorted. "Because we want this thing between us to be authentic. Don't come on too strong, but also don't ignore me."

"Let me get this straight." Beyond annoyed by his dictatorship so far, I swiveled in my seat as much as the seat belt would allow. "I'm to be by your side in a look-but-don't-touch-unless-you-initiate-it manner. And I would list the rest of your rules, but they're all stupid. Why don't you just bring a puppy to school? I'm not sure there would be much difference."

"That's how we're going to do things. I'm trying to help you. But if you want to be a bitch about it, then we can call it off. Or we can work together, and you can return to who you're supposed to be without stupid shit happening to you at school or vandalism at home."

"Really. And who am I supposed to be?" *Aside from your temporary fake girlfriend?*

"Someone who takes a bad situation and turns it in her favor."

"And dating you is in my favor?"

He pulled into the school's lot and parked. "It is."

Fuck, fine. He was right, but I did not want to admit it.

Damon came around and opened my door. When I got out, he clasped my hand in his, and we walked up the front steps to the school entrance, past others who'd arrived or were procrastinating going in, then to my locker together. I felt all the eyes on us, and I tipped my chin a little higher. *Screw them.* I was almost on board with Damon's plan. Not the rules. "Dictator" and "alpha asshole" were a few of the terms that came to mind about those.

People filled the halls, and many rubbernecked as we walked in together. I smirked then quickly wiped the expression from my face. I didn't care what people thought, but I wanted them to leave me alone.

Damon walked me to class, and when I got out, he was waiting for me. I caught up quickly to the theme of the day. He would stick to me like glue when he could. When we went to chemistry together, his arm snaked around my waist and pulled me close. That I didn't have a problem with. It was nice.

I wanted to laugh at how people reacted—even his cousins. We passed Phoenix in the hall, and Damon fist-bumped him. A curious look sent my way was the only acknowledgment of my presence.

In class, Damon sat close, occasionally playing with my hair while the teacher droned on. Something about how a guy did that felt amazing. I was almost in a drugged comma by the time he stopped. It took everything in me not to turn to him and demand more. But that would have been weird, so I remained quiet—which was the other thing going on between us. We didn't talk much. That was fine with me. Maybe. Yes. It was. We weren't friends. But by lunchtime, I was exhausted, my body in a constant state of awareness from his nearness.

I wasn't sure what my experience in the cafeteria would hold. I walked in without Damon. Shocking, I know. And I hated to say it, but in a way, I missed his presence. I was getting used to his constant touches and staying glued to his side as he talked to his friends. It felt weird to be alone. He'd even told one or two of the footballers that I was his girlfriend and that if he caught them checking me out again, they would find themselves facing him in the Ring. I'd had to work hard not to roll my eyes at that one. Especially when the big footballers looked like they would piss themselves. So funny.

I kept my face expressionless as I got into line. I chose a salad and an apple then balanced a bottle of water precariously on the tray. I scanned the area where I usually sat. I found nothing strange there, and the tension between my shoulders eased. Damon sat with his cousins, Jessica, Tracey, and a few other girls I had no interest in getting to know. Gia had been half a dozen people behind me in line to get her food. I wondered where she would sit. Probably with them as she'd been doing. All good. I was fine on my own.

When I was a few steps from my table, Damon's voice cut through the noise. "Come sit with me, Sky."

It wasn't a question, and I wanted to turn and give him the finger. But part of the deal was to follow his lead. *For now.* He would hear about it from me after school. That was the only thing that enabled me to keep the barely restrained sneer off my face as I changed directions and went to his table, where the Elite reigned.

Shane moved over, forcing Tracey and the other girls to do so as well, eliciting several glares from them. I almost wanted to laugh at what they would face soon because Damon was proving to be quite the guard dog, at least with the football players. And that shit had spread fast. I'd received no more leers from any of the overinflated-egocentric athletes.

I set down my tray and climbed over the bench between Damon and Shane. Phoenix sat on Damon's other side, and he winked then went back to eating his sandwich.

"Hey, gorgeous." Damon sank his hand into my hair, angling my head for a slow, seductive kiss.

When I came up for air, my brain was officially scrambled. Gia stood at the end of the table, and if smoke could have come out of her ears, it would have. One of the cheerleaders scooted over for her, but Damon's head snapped up.

He fixed the cheerleader with a look that would make anyone run for cover. "No."

The girl moved back to her place then turned to the person next to her, avoiding eye contact with everyone else.

Then Damon focused that intensity on Gia. His arm slid down my arm to my waist, drawing me closer so not even an inch separated us. "You're not welcome at this table anymore."

I jerked in his embrace, automatically reacting, my mouth parting to come to her defense. His eyes met mine, hard and unyielding, then I remembered—the T-shirts, the rumors, the laughter, her shoving me in the hallway, ridiculing me at work, the graffiti on our garage door. Everything in me hardened. It was a bitter lesson for Gia to learn, but she'd made her own bed.

Gia's face flamed beneath her olive skin. She aimed a vicious glare at me before she went to our old table. I didn't care. I scooted away from Damon enough to dig into my salad and listened to the chatter at the table, comfortable not engaging. I wasn't there to make new temporary friends, because that was all they would be. And the girls were vipers, not what I needed in my life.

I wasn't proud of how things had gone with Gia, but I was resigned. I could only take so much abuse. The excuses I'd made in my head for her behavior didn't hold up anymore.

The rest of the day went pretty much the same. I didn't mind the security of Damon's presence. No one dared mess with me when he was clearly marking me as his. Then there were the sweet kisses in the hallway now and then. He kept them PG, which made me happy. I'd already been labeled a slut by Gia, and I didn't want to give the label credibility.

By the time school was over, I was exhausted from playing a role I knew wasn't real. The constant touching had kept my body in a state of arousal from when we'd first arrived at school, and I was glad to climb into his SUV and close my eyes as he drove me to work.

We pulled into the restaurant parking lot, and I unhooked my seat belt. I turned to him, one hand on the door. Damon stared straight ahead, not making eye contact.

"Thanks for—"

He grimaced. "Get out."

His voice was harsh, and I had whiplash from how convincing he'd been at school.

I wouldn't just take that lying down. "Fuck you." I jumped out of the car, slamming the door without a backward glance.

What the hell was that? I knew he had to get back for football practice, but seriously? I shook my head, feeling foolish. I shouldn't be surprised. He wasn't my boyfriend. The thing between us was fake, and his response was probably meant as a reminder to us both.

Leaving the bullshit in the parking lot, I pasted a smile on my face as I walked in and said hi to Rachel, the hostess, and the other servers before going into the bathroom and changing. When I was dressed in the Chicks-N-Wings uniform, I hung my backpack in the back room and got to work on the section the hostess had assigned me.

Work went well, and I forgot about Damon's strange reaction and how weird school had been until toward the end of my shift, when Gia walked in with her two new friends. I was mildly surprised they hadn't turned into frenemies yet. But maybe they thought she would emerge on top of the obvious love-triangle spat among her, Damon, and me.

I groaned when they were seated in my section. Gia

smoothed her shorn and straightened blond hair while Tina laughed evilly. It wasn't going to go well, and I seriously considered quitting on the spot. I had enough money for Mom's birthday, and the abuse from that table wasn't something I wanted to experience again.

Instead of walking out, I sucked it up and pasted on a fake smile. Notebook and pen in hand, I stood before them. "What can I get you guys to drink?"

"Nothing, whore." Gia's voice screeched through the restaurant.

"You need to leave, Gia." I was done taking her shit. I owed her more than I could ever repay, but what she was doing had to stop.

Hatred flashed in her big brown eyes. She was the one who had chosen a boy over our friendship. I wanted to remind her of that, but it wasn't the time or place.

"I wouldn't let you bring me anything you could contaminate anyway." She shoved her way out of the booth and rammed into me.

My face flamed as I stumbled back. Her cohorts cackled, following her dramatic exit.

"Slut."

I didn't know if that was Tina or Rebecca. I didn't care because I'd caught a glimpse of the parking lot as the manager hurried over to me. The car was back. Fear raced over my body, chasing away any embarrassment or hurt from what Gia had said and done. I had bigger problems than the feud between us.

"Are you all right, Skylar?" James's light touch at my elbow guided me into Gia's vacated chair. "Don't worry. Those girls will be banned for their behavior."

I tore my gaze from the parking lot and met James's kind brown eyes. He was a giant teddy bear who worked most of the afternoon shifts.

"I'm fine. Sorry about the scene."

"Do not apologize. I won't tolerate bullying, and those girls were clearly in the wrong. But you look shaken." He scanned the restaurant. "We're slow today. Do you need to take the night off?" He glanced at his watch. "You only have an hour left anyway."

"Yeah, if you don't mind." I appreciated it more than he would ever know, and with how complicated things were, I also planned on turning in my resignation later. I scanned the floor. "Will the others be able to cover my tables?"

"I'll cover them and set aside your tips for you. Don't worry about a thing."

"Thank you." I hurried to the back room and texted Damon, asking him to pick me up. Football practice would be long over. I only hoped he was by his phone and not sparring or working out. Seconds later, he replied that he was on his way.

I sagged against the back of the staff couch and waited until he texted that he was outside. With my backpack over my shoulder, I thanked James again and said goodbye to Rachel. Then I burst out of the restaurant and into Damon's car, scanning the parking lot as I shut the door. The overhead lights lit the lot well enough that I would have seen anything unusual. The car was gone.

I felt ridiculous, like the girl who cried wolf, and would not tell Damon. He studied me before pulling away, and I let my head fall back against the leather headrest, closing my eyes.

Did I imagine it?

CHAPTER NINE

DAMON

#UpCloseandPersonal

Sky trembled as I pulled out of the restaurant's parking lot. Something was wrong. If it was because of Gia, all bets were off. I would go after the girl. Part of me felt bad that I might have contributed to her stress, since I'd acted like an ass when I'd dropped her off earlier. I couldn't separate the fake from the real part of being with her during school, and it was messing with my head.

With Sky, things moved too fast. My mind warred with how much I wanted her but shouldn't, and since I did in such an overwhelming way, it proved I was more like my dad than I'd thought. Because he'd wanted Raelyn to the point of Mom's self-destruction.

"I don't want to go home."

"Did something happen?" Fierce protectiveness roared through me, overriding all other thoughts. Sky wasn't mine to own or anyone's, but it felt like she was.

"I don't want to talk about it." Wide blue eyes met mine, her voice a soft caress I couldn't deny.

I changed direction and took her to the academy. The vulnerability vibrating around her needed to be addressed, and I planned to do something about it. After parking, I brought her into the school with the keys my brother had passed down to me. We walked silently through the halls then down to the basement, where I flipped on the lights, illuminating the sparring mats.

"Why are we here?" She toed the mat, her face pale even in the dimly lit area.

"This is where I spar with my cousins." I stepped onto the mat.

"Yeah, I know. You told me last time."

I waved her forward. "I thought I would show you a few moves."

Interest sparked in the blue depth of her eyes. "Oh, okay." She stepped onto the mat and faced me.

"We're going to use a scenario that you're being attacked, then I'll teach you what to do about it." I wanted to impart the basics before getting to anything else. "You want to concentrate on your attacker's most vulnerable areas—eyes, nose, throat, and groin." The corners of her mouth twitched, and I grinned back. "I already know what you're imagining."

"I get to take a free shot at your groin?"

And I was right. "Hardly."

Smiling, she shrugged. "This sounds like fun."

I chuckled, happy to see her a little more relaxed. "I'll explain the moves, then we'll practice them." I took her through an elbow strike and explained how to position her car keys between her fingers as a weapon, how to deliver a palm strike to the nose, and how to escape from several holds.

Then we got to the fun part—practicing. She tried combinations of palm strikes and groin shots that I blocked. I showed her how to block punches, sweep a leg, use her body to strengthen her holds, and avoid letting her smaller size become a disadvantage. We reviewed them and the restrained positions until she improved enough that I was confident with her form. She would continue to improve, but already, her confidence seemed better.

We were breathing hard by the end of the lesson, and all the touching drove me crazy. She smelled incredible and felt so good in my arms. The last time I'd come down there with her, I could have done things to her, but she hadn't liked the basement.

"Are you ready to go?"

She shook her head slowly.

Fuck it. I wanted her, and I closed the short distance between us. Grasping the edge of her work shirt, I eased it up while watching for any signs of her resistance. She gave none as she helped shimmy out of her clothes until she stood naked before me.

Awareness over anything but Sky was quickly becoming a problem, and I pulled a condom out of my jeans pocket, stripped my clothes, and put it on. There wouldn't be time later, not with the mounting desire crackling through the air. I was utterly addicted to her and needed to be inside her like my next breath.

I was so turned on that going slowly wasn't an option. With no clothes separating us, I cupped her ass and lifted her. Her legs automatically wrapped around me, and I backed her against a wall where a few mats hung. Pinning her between the mat and me, I took her lips in a desperate kiss, devouring her them, ruthlessly invading her mouth until she moaned.

A tremor went through her body as I slid my fingers down her silky skin to brush in a teasing caress over her clit. Met by her warm, wet heat, I slipped my finger in, my thumb circling her clit as I pumped inside her, then I curled my finger until she panted.

"Damon," she moaned. "Stop tormenting me."

By the way her legs tightened around me, urging me closer, I knew she was close. Withdrawing my fingers to the sweet sounds of her protests, I aligned the tip of my cock with her entrance and slanted my mouth over hers.

Her hands tangled in my hair, tugging the strands as she kissed me with the same need. She nipped at my lip then ran her tongue over it, and I lost it. Positioned at her slick entrance, I thrust in. Her head fell back on a low moan, and I wrapped my hand around the nape of her neck. The other gripped her ass as I drove deep. Her hips tilted, and she met my furious pace.

I grazed my teeth over the soft skin from her neck to her shoulder, eliciting a whimper as I increased the pressure. A mark would form there, and I fucking loved it. She arched against me, and a wave of lust drove me to go harder, faster until her body convulsed around me, and she cried out.

Two more pumps, and I followed her, spilling deep inside her. I leaned into her, bracing one arm on the wall as we caught our breath.

Then she laughed, and the sound was so carefree and sensual that my mouth watered. A fine sheen of sweat coated her, and her firm breasts glistened, tempting me to take her nipples into my mouth and worship every inch of her again. She was so beautiful.

We both groaned as I pulled out, and she slid her legs down. I made sure she had her footing before releasing her to dispose of the condom. Afterward, I ran my hands through my hair, somewhat shaken up at how insatiable she made me feel.

It was getting late, and we'd been in the basement almost two hours. "I should probably get you home."

Her teeth caught her lower lip. Her hungry eyes held mine as she released it then shook her head. "I don't think so."

Goddamn. That was all it took, and I was on her, that time taking her down to the mat on top of our pile of clothes.

It was another hour before I brought her home. And later, in my room, after I realized she'd left her backpack in my car, I texted her. When she responded, I called her—something I'd never done for any girl but Sky.

We talked for an hour until she was tired enough to sleep. And when I hung up, I realized that I was well and truly fucked because one touch of Sky's hand could bring me to my knees.

CHAPTER TEN

SKYLAR

#SecretsRevealed

After Damon dropped me off, I went into the house to find Mom pacing with the phone pressed to her ear. Worry lined her face around her mouth with pinched creases between her brows. Whoever she was talking to made her upset.

I sat on the couch, waiting to find out what was happening, even as the thought of the mystery car hovered in my mind. When Mom turned and saw me, she jumped and seemed more nervous.

"I've got to go." Her eyes held mine. "Can we talk about this later?"

The other person must have agreed because she hung up. "What did you hear?"

Strange. "Nothing. I just got home."

"Okay." Mom tried to smile but failed miserably.

Something terrible was going on, and from the stubborn set of her shoulders, I knew she wasn't ready to share it with me.

"It's getting late. You should probably go to bed," she said.

I didn't push her. She would talk to me when she was ready,

so I got up and did as she'd suggested. After I closed the door to my room and flopped onto my bed, a deep sense of loneliness invaded the bubble Damon and I had managed to create. It was times like that when I missed Gia the most. We used to talk about everything. We had probably stayed on the phone hundreds of nights until one or both of us had fallen asleep, which had usually been close to when the sun came up.

I took my phone from my pocket and palmed it, wanting badly to call her. When it buzzed, I hoped for a misguided second that it was her. It wasn't. Damon had texted that I had left my backpack in his SUV. I replied that I would just get it the next day.

A soft knock sounded at my door, distracting me before it opened. Mom came into my room, leaning back against the doorjamb, nervously twisting a few strands of hair. "I thought I would knock. I didn't want to get another eyeful."

I scrunched my nose. "Not funny."

"Sorry." Her gaze shot to the window. The curtains were closed, and it seemed to settle her slightly. She sighed then pushed away from the wall and joined me on my bed, where she studied me. "Is everything okay?"

"Not really." I sat up and crossed my legs. "Gia won't forgive me."

"I'm sorry, honey." She squeezed my hand. "I'm sure she'll come around. You guys have been friends for too long to let a guy come between you."

"Maybe." *Doubtful.* "What's going on with you?"

She'd come into my room, which meant she must be ready to talk. She visibly tensed and clasped her hands in her lap, but I didn't miss how they trembled.

"Your dad will be released in under three weeks."

"We have a restraining order, right?" *Do those even work?*

"Yeah. He isn't allowed to contact us or come within a

hundred yards, but if he tries, you need to let me know immediately."

"What'll happen if he does try?" Because the car—someone was watching us. It had to do with him.

"I'll have him arrested." She pasted on that fake smile again, making me even more anxious. "I'm going to try to get some sleep. I've got an early client tomorrow."

"Good night, Mom."

"Night, honey." She shut the door quietly behind her.

I couldn't shake the ominous feeling about Dad being released. *And if he does approach us, what will happen?* I was pretty sure I knew—for Mom, anyway. It made me super anxious, and I wanted to ensure I could protect her and myself if he tried to get near us. The stuff Damon had shown me was my best bet, and I texted him asking for a couple more fighting lessons.

He didn't reply. Instead, he called me. I answered on the first ring.

"What do you need the lessons for?"

Getting right to the point. Too bad I didn't want to tell him. "I just like knowing that if a situation comes up, I can handle myself."

Silence hung between us for about two seconds until he called my bluff. "Try again."

Asshole. "That's a perfectly good reason."

"It is, but I don't believe it's the right one. You've been nervous. Tell me what's going on."

In the short time I'd gotten to know Damon a little better, I'd learned how stubborn and relentless he could be—and smart. Besides, the deep-seated need to talk about it festered in me. "My dad's going to be released from prison in less than three weeks, and my mom's a wreck about it. What he did to her was why he went to jail."

"What happened?" His voice was soft, luring me into a sense

of security, but it wouldn't have taken much to get me there in the first place.

"He beat my mom almost to death. I don't remember that part, only running through our backyard and into Gia's tree-house to hide. I was little, and when she found me, she brought me to her parents because I was bleeding. Her parents saved my mom. If it weren't for Gia and her family, I don't think my mom would be here today."

"Did he hit you?" He growled the words, but I wasn't scared of Damon.

"I don't know. Well, yes, he did, but I remember nothing about that day except running outside and to her yard."

"What's the situation when he's out of jail? Will he live with you?"

"I don't have any information on where he'll go. But we have a restraining order out on him. He isn't supposed to come near Mom or me."

"That's why Gia's friendship is so important to you, isn't it?"

"Yeah. She saved us and never told anyone at school either." It felt so good to talk about it with someone and to have Damon realize why I'd put up with how horrible she'd been to me. "So, will you help me?"

"Yes."

I relaxed against my pillow as we made plans to spar together. I felt like I could breathe again because, with Damon's instruction, I could keep Mom and myself safe.

CHAPTER ELEVEN

DAMON

#FridayNightLights

The bench. I couldn't believe it. Coach benched me for missing one day of practice when I'd helped Sky. He needed me, and I had no doubt he would find that out. I wasn't the only furious one. Phoenix had had words with Coach already. To my cousin, the game was his life, his future. And I got it because it was the same way for my brother. I needed it, too, but if I didn't get drafted, I would find another fulfilling career, and I suspected Shane was the same way.

My imminent future wasn't the pressing problem. It was the game. I wanted in as badly as Phoenix wanted me there, and another wave of anger ripped through me at my ineligible status.

With me riding the bench, the second-string running back was in. As the game started, I ground my teeth. Cole and Riley were in the stands with Sky. Cole's team had a bye week, and they'd decided to come home just for the game. Of course, that shit had to happen when my brother was back.

We had the ball, and when it snapped to Phoenix, he read the field. Shane was tied up with two guys on his ass. The ball left Phoenix's hands in a beautiful spiral right to Johnston's chest, which it bounced off. I launched myself from the bench and paced along the sidelines. Time and again, Johnston, the second-string running back, dropped the ball, looked behind him instead of up, ran short, or fumbled. It was a nightmare, and the entire offensive line was frustrated. Shane had caught two, but the other team was on him like glue.

Our defense did its job and held the line for the most part. But our opponents were up by fourteen points. It would ruin our undefeated position, something I knew Coach wouldn't want either.

Before halftime and during, I hounded Coach, pleading my case. He finally let me in, and I did what I did best—ran unpredictable routes that the other team wouldn't expect, became a wall for Shane when he needed one, and scored the winning touchdown. As we celebrated on the field, my gaze found and held Sky's, and I waved her down.

The team was at the bench and heading in when she got to the field. In those few seconds, before I had to go to the locker room with everyone else, I kissed her—in front of everyone. She went with it, playing her role for the school to get Gia and her groupies off Sky's back. But it didn't feel fake anymore, and surprisingly, that didn't bother me.

I had to leave her with Cole and Riley when I went to the locker room with the team. Coach's speech was longer than usual because of the mistakes made. As soon as he finished, I hurried to get showered and dressed. When I walked out of there, I found Sky leaning against the brick wall, waiting for me.

We had a part to play with my fake relationship scheme, but I didn't mind, and with each casual touch, it moved to the near side of real. Part of me liked it a lot. But I wouldn't do anything further about it. We were temporary. And that was how it had to be.

Cole and Riley headed back to Thane, and Sky and I got in my SUV.

"Want to come over?" I asked.

"Yeah." She grinned, but then it slipped. "Hey, no one else knows about my dad except for Gia and her family. I would appreciate it if you didn't tell anyone."

"Why would I?" It pissed me off that she'd even felt the need to mention it.

She shrugged, and I turned at the light, heading toward my house.

"I didn't think you would," she said. "It's just one of those things you say to feel better about the situation."

I had no comment. It was insulting. But I took her to my house anyway. And when we got there, Raelyn and my dad were home. I introduced them to Sky, hoping to move past them quickly, but it didn't work that way.

"Skylar the writer?" Raelyn asked.

Her cheeks pinkened. "I guess? I write for the academy's blog."

"Well, we owe you." Raelyn grinned. "Riley told me what you did for her with the articles her senior year. If you need anything, please let me know."

"Thank you."

"Good game tonight," Dad said.

I grunted and pulled Sky toward the basement.

When we got there, I turned on the TV and pulled up an action movie, feeling her gaze the entire time. "What?"

"What's the deal with you and your parents?"

"*Parent.* Raelyn is not my mom." I turned and pinned her with a look as she held up her hands.

"Right. I get that. But something's going on there. What's the problem? And before you completely shut me out, remember that I told you about my deal."

"Fine." *What will it hurt if I tell her about my family drama?* Hers wasn't much better. "You know Cole and I are close."

"Yeah." She kicked off her shoes and tucked her legs under her on the leather couch, getting comfortable.

"Cole knew things about our dad—his cheating." I frowned, still angry that I'd refused to see it. "And I... didn't."

Sky waited for me to continue, saying nothing.

"My dad and Riley's mom met a long time ago, and he cheated on my mom with her. It tore our mom up, not to mention exacerbated the depression she struggled with."

"That's not good."

"No. Things were difficult at home. The whole school knows how we found Mom one weekend, surrounded by empty pill bottles after she had us deliver a letter to our father. But what isn't common knowledge is Raelyn. She was there when we gave Dad that note. She's been the one between them all along."

Sky worried her bottom lip, and I continued when I felt no judgment from her.

"Then she showed up here, and Dad had her come live with us. There's that, and then he went and married her."

"Raelyn being in town last year was why Cole gave Riley hell?"

"Yes. I didn't always get along with my mom, but if Raelyn hadn't come around, I feel like Mom would still be here. When my brother told me everything, all the pieces clicked into place. Cole's made peace with what happened. I have not."

Sky nodded then looked down at her hands. Her reaction, the way she didn't offer sympathy but accepted what I was going through, eased something inside me, and a portion of the ever-present anger fizzled out.

CHAPTER TWELVE

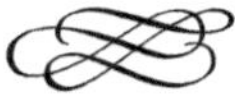

SKYLAR

#RunningShoes

Damon dropped me off after we hung out and talked in his basement, which was more like a luxury apartment with a leather sectional, giant TV, pool table, and bar. My entire house could probably fit in there.

I was surprised by how much I liked spending time with him, when he wasn't being an asshole anyway. We were getting closer, but I refused to read into it. The deal was to fool everyone at school into thinking we were dating, and that was it, even if it seemed like we'd become friends.

When I walked into my dimly lit living room, Mom was chewing on one of her nails, her leg bouncing restlessly.

As soon as she saw me, she leaped to her feet. "We're moving."

"What? When?" I stopped short, shock running through me like a riptide. "Did something happen?"

"We'll move in two weeks. That way I can get everything wrapped up with work." She shoved her dark hair from her face, her eyes wild with terror. "I've looked at this scenario from every angle, and it always comes down to the same conclusion. He'll come here."

"Well, he knows where we live, since this was his house too. But I thought he couldn't."

"I don't think a piece of paper will matter to him. If we stay, we could risk our lives, and I can't take that chance."

I sat on the couch, my legs suddenly shaky. "I don't think running is the answer."

"At the trial, when he was sentenced, he made threats."

I tried to defuse her panic, for both our sakes. "That was a long time ago. Maybe he's over it now."

She snorted, grabbed a letter off the peninsula, and handed it to me. "Nothing makes a guy forget like time spent in prison."

Her joke fell flat and only managed to freak me out more.

I glanced at the envelope, noting that it was from my dad while in prison. I took it out and unfolded it, feeling like I was opening Pandora's box. I read the handwritten words while Mom waited. On the surface, the letter sounded fine, but it was a thinly veiled threat saying that he would come for us "to make up for all the years he'd lost in prison."

I rechecked the envelope. "This came today?" At Mom's nod, I relaxed a little. "We can take this to the cops. I bet they'll increase security around us or maybe even revoke his release." That last one was weak, but it would've been nice.

"No. The cops didn't save us when it was happening years ago. The domestic calls did nothing to stop him. It was Gia's family who saved us."

Her words were a gut punch of guilt.

"We can go north or east. You've never even seen the snow." Mom injected a sense of excitement into her voice that neither of us felt. "It'll be an adventure. We'll build snowmen, learn how to ski or ice skate, and drink hot chocolate in front of a fire. It'll be great."

"Okay." I choked on the word.

"You're on board?" She grabbed my hands, holding them tightly.

"Yes, of course."

He hadn't killed her last time. I didn't want to take a chance that he would succeed if I didn't agree and leave. I told her I was tired and wanted to sleep, since we didn't have all the details about where we were going yet, only that his release date was a Tuesday—in two freaking weeks. Mom seemed relieved, and I slipped from the family room to my bedroom, sending Damon a text that we needed to talk once I was alone. I needed him. My fingers hovered over the keys until I gave in and added a 911.

CHAPTER THIRTEEN

DAMON

#GTFO

I was in my SUV and on the road the second after I got Sky's 911 text. I didn't even recognize myself anymore. All I could think about was getting to her and making sure she was okay. I flew down the street until I came to her street, where I forced myself to pull into her driveway without coming to a screeching halt.

The next thing I knew, I was at her window, tapping on the pane, begging for entry. I needed to see her. I suspected it was the only way the cloying panic would recede.

Sky peeked through the curtains, and when she saw me, she whipped them open. After unlocking the window, she pushed it up.

I climbed through and gripped her shoulders. All I could think about was getting to her, feeling her in my arms, and never wanting to let her go. That kind of need wasn't like me at all, and deep inside, part of me fought for it to be. "What's wrong?"

Tremors ran through her, and I knew that whatever had

happened was significant. I drew her close, and she wrapped her arms around my waist, laying her head on my chest.

"We're moving."

"In your senior year? Why?" It made no sense. *Is this because of that bitch Gia?*

"Because my mom's scared. My dad gets out of jail two weeks from Tuesday. And she thinks he'll come after us."

Fuck. I was at a crossroads, and I didn't like it. I ran my hand down her long, silky hair, analyzing the very real dilemma in my mind. The last thing I wanted was for Sky to move away, but letting her know how I felt wasn't an option.

The noose tightened around my throat. If I told her how much I cared about her and thought about her constantly, she would gain too much power. And unequal power in a relationship was a very bad thing—it struck a chord that pointed at what my dad had held over my mom.

He hadn't cared as much, if at all, and had stepped out on her, leaving her destroyed but unable to quit him. My dad had screwed around on her because Mom would never have done anything about it. Until she did.

Either way, the control Sky or I would have over one another was too much like my parents, and I refused to engage in that. But I also couldn't let her leave without one last memory. I tangled my hands in the hair at her nape, tilting her head back.

I kissed her, memorizing the way she melted against me, coaxing her soft moan as I explored her mouth, reveling in how her hands traced over my chest until her arms wrapped around my neck.

I backed her toward the bed.

She tore her lips from mine. "What are you doing?" Desire looked incredible on Sky with her swollen lips and flushed cheeks.

"Giving you something to remember me by."

She flattened her hands on my chest and shoved me. "Get the fuck out."

Shit. That went horribly wrong, and panic shot through me with the thought of never seeing her again. "I'm sorry." I ran my fingers along her cheek and tucked her hair behind her ear. I never apologized to a girl. The person I was becoming was completely foreign to me, but having Sky walk out of my life was the greater fear. "I didn't mean it like that."

She crossed her arms over her chest and glared. "Get out, Damon. And leave me alone."

My skin felt tight, and I slicked my tongue over my teeth, mind racing for the right words to calm her down so she might let me stay. "That's the thing, Sky. I can't leave you alone. You called, and I came right over."

"Right, because I was vulnerable, and you thought I would be an easy fuck. Not because you were worried about me or wanted to be here for emotional support"—her finger stabbed me in the chest—"or listen to me."

I held my arms out, encompassing the space around us, doing everything I could not to let my frustration show in my expression. "I am here."

"Not the same thing." She shook her head then pointed at the window. "Please just go."

I didn't want to, but I couldn't do anything to convince her to let me stay, so I climbed out the same way I'd gotten in.

But when I got to my SUV, a car drove by slowly without its headlights on. That had to be the car Sky had told me about, and I hurried to follow. I turned the corner, the car was nowhere to be seen, and the threat to her safety solidified. Maybe her moving wasn't such a bad idea.

Then why do I hate it with every fiber of my being?

CHAPTER FOURTEEN

SKYLAR

#FakeDating

With a sigh, I grabbed my bag containing sunscreen and a towel. This wasn't a good idea. The reflection in the mirror didn't look like me, but I'd wanted a change, even if it was a minor one. It was a compromise of sorts. The black bikini I wore reflected who I was and gave me a modicum of comfort. But the cover-up wasn't me. White, sheer, and sexy, it fell to midthigh and left nothing to the imagination. Black oversized sunglasses and my hair in a messy bun at the top of my head completed the look.

I slipped my feet into a pair of sandals and went to answer the door.

Part of me wondered why I was bothering if Mom and I were moving. But then, I still had hope that things would change and we wouldn't have to go, which was why I had decided to move forward like nothing was wrong.

I'd kept Damon waiting for a hot minute. It was necessary. We needed to sell our first fake date outside of school, which meant I had to get my head in the game. I was ready. Or as ready as I would ever be.

I opened the door, already tensed for what I would see. He didn't disappoint with his blue-and-gray board shorts and a tight dark-gray shirt that outlined every curve and muscle dip. It was going to be a long day. A wolfish grin slowly curved Damon's mouth, and I grimaced from the heat of it.

My hand flattened on his chest, and I pushed. "We have to go, right?"

If we stayed, all the effort I'd taken to put my outfit together would be ruined. It would be on the floor instead, along with his clothes.

"Today has a purpose, one you insisted on," I reminded him.

He stepped back, silently waiting for me to close and lock the door. When his hand found mine, I jumped.

Blue eyes watched me. "Are you nervous?"

"Yeah." It was weird. "I'm not sure why."

"It'll be fun. I promise. Phoenix and Shane are already there, and from what they told me, about thirty other people too."

"Great. That's reassuring."

A shiver raced through me, and Damon chuckled. If my friends were there, I would be more comfortable with the crowd of vultures, but I doubted they would be. Maybe Tucker. He hung with that crowd on occasion because of wrestling.

Damon opened the passenger door for me, and I climbed into his black Range Rover. After getting in and pressing the start button, he pulled out of the driveway and onto the road heading toward the cove. Music pumped through the speakers, and I enjoyed the reprieve from conversation.

Twenty minutes later, we pulled into the cove's packed parking lot. We got out, and Damon clasped my hand in his again. He led me to where Phoenix sat on a towel on the small sandy section that led into the water. People jumped from the cliffs, some screaming as they hurtled themselves off the rocky ledge.

"Hey, Sky." Phoenix shielded his eyes as he peered up at me. "Are you gonna jump?"

"No." I shuddered. "Not in a million years. Falling to my death isn't my goal in life."

"It's not bad if you pick one of the lower ledges." Phoenix grinned before his gaze shifted past me. "Incoming."

Damon's arm slipped around my waist, and he pulled me close as Shane and Tracey strolled up. Stunning as usual, Tracey was picture ready in her hot-pink Brazilian bikini with a sheer white wrap tied low on her hips. A few others moved to join, adding to the group around Phoenix.

Tracey's nose wrinkled as she skimmed me from head to foot. She didn't bother me. I leaned against Damon more, wrapping my arm around his waist, too, and did my best to ignore her. People swam in the cove a safe distance from where the jumpers landed. The water was much warmer than if we'd gone to the beach.

Damon tapped one of the football players' shoulders. "Move over."

The guy grinned, said hi to me, then got the entire group to shift, making room for Damon and me to spread our towels by Phoenix.

Shane hooked his finger in the loose knot of Tracey's wrap and pulled, letting it float to the sand in a fall of sheer fabric. He grabbed her by the waist, and she shrieked and laughed as he lifted her off her feet and waded into the water.

I sat, legs stretched out, on the towel Damon had spread so I was buffered between him and Phoenix. I crossed my ankles and leaned back on my hands as the sun beat down, warming my exposed skin.

"Thane's coach will be at the game against Mammoth Academy the weekend Cole is coming home. It's some extended weekend for them, so the timing was good." Phoenix's words were quiet so only we heard him.

"We're already in." Damon leaned around me to talk to his cousin. "So, why's that a big deal?"

"Because we don't have guaranteed starting positions." Phoenix's brows furrowed. "Every chance he sees us is an opportunity."

Damon grinned. "And you're letting me know this so I don't fuck it up?"

"Yeah." Stormy silver eyes latched onto mine. "What about you, Sky? Are you going to interview him for the blog?"

Not a bad idea. "I just might. How did you come by this information?"

"He emailed me. I thought I would do my brother and cousin a solid."

"Pretty damn nice of you." While I despised athletes, I couldn't deny that a few of them were growing on me. But even at gunpoint, I wouldn't admit it. "And also interesting that you were the only one who got that email."

Damon snorted. "He's a hotshot QB. None of us are surprised. Have you seen the starting quarterback at Thane?"

"Ah, no. I can't say I have, since I don't watch sports in my spare time."

"No?" Phoenix's head tilted. "We need to fix that, D."

"Sky's not into sports, which you know." Damon rummaged through his bag. He pulled out bottled water and offered it to me.

I took it, and he grabbed two more and tossed one to Phoenix.

"Then why are you writing the sports section?"

Damon already knew Stephanie had assigned the football games to me, but I shouldn't be surprised that Phoenix didn't. All that meant was he didn't tell his cousins everything. I was sure my lack of interest in sports ranked at the bottom of what he considered conversation worthy.

"I write what the editor assigns," I stated.

"Oh, that kind of sucks."

"Right?" I unscrewed the water and sipped before putting the cap back on.

"What would you rather write about?" Damon wrapped his arms around his bent knees and focused entirely on me.

"I would rather tackle more serious issues, like problems with the school board, how standardized testing should or shouldn't be a factor for college acceptance, trauma and how it affects students, things like that."

"If not you, who is? I've seen articles on those topics, but I haven't paid attention to who's writing them," Damon asked.

Someone looped Phoenix into a conversation on his other side, and I turned more toward Damon. "Marc Hamilton. Our editor, Stephanie, is dating him."

"I see. He gets to pick whatever he's interested in, then."

"Yep." I popped the *p*. "It's annoying but not horrible. I've learned a lot about football since I started covering the home games."

"It probably helps that Riley comes on occasion." Damon downed a third of his water. "I'm not surprised you two are friends."

I shrugged. "Riley's cool. I liked her when I met her last year. And all that crap your brother did, the ostracizing and unleashing the vipers, didn't faze her at all."

"Nah." He laughed. "She's tough. And she gave it back as good as he dished it out."

"I could see her doing that. Are you looking forward to going to school with them next year?"

"Yeah. I fucking miss the hell out of my brother. It's been great that he's come home for some of our games. And the year is going by pretty fast."

"You're planning on the NFL too." I didn't need to ask it like a question. I already knew. "It would be so crazy if the four of you went pro." For some reason, the thought of it didn't make me want to gag. In my eyes, Damon was becoming a human being rather than just what he represented—an athlete. The thought alone should have made me run away, but it didn't.

"I guess. But the likelihood of us being on the same team is slim. We've grown up together, and they're all my best friends. I can't imagine being apart." He shook his head, seeming to pull himself from his thoughts. "It'll work out. Whatever happens. Who knows? I may not even go into the NFL."

"Really? What are you thinking about majoring in?"

His features hardened, and he shifted his gaze from me to the water. "Corporate law."

"Like your dad?"

"That was the plan."

I wanted to ask more, but his body language said he was done with the topic, and I didn't particularly want him storming off and leaving me with a bunch of snarly girls who would tell me I didn't belong. I was well aware it wasn't my crowd. I scanned the sea of faces again for Tucker, hoping he'd arrived so I would have someone to talk to when Damon wasn't around.

Damon stood abruptly and held out his hand. "Come on. Let's go swim."

After getting to my feet, pulling off my cover-up, and dropping that and my sunglasses on the towel, I took his hand. His large fingers curled around mine, and he tugged me close. We had done so much touching lately. It made me feel claimed in the most stomach-flipping way. I should hate it. But a secret part of me didn't.

Damon walked backward into the water, pulling me with him. That wolfish grin curved his lips, and I shivered in anticipation. We moved far to the left, away from the cliff divers, who needed space to land.

I swirled my fingertips in the water when Damon stopped. It was up to his waist and higher on me.

"Looking hot, Sky."

The corners of my mouth twitched. "Not helping, Damon."

"Oh, I think it is." He pulled me close, and I looped my arms around his neck. "We're at a cove party, and everyone here is watching."

"Sure." I'd seen the looks.

A few girls had lifted a hand in a small wave when we'd first entered the water. But plenty of them were still furious. They would give me a hard time during school or at work.

"It's only partially working. Your fan club, or maybe it's Gia's now, isn't buying it," I said.

"We're just getting started."

His gaze dropped to my lips, and I stiffened.

"We need to keep this PG, Romeo."

He chuckled before he brushed his lips against mine, teasing me. I knew what he tasted like, what he could do to me with one kiss. Heat built in my stomach, spreading through my body.

"Don't worry. I've got your back."

I melted. He'd said what I needed to hear most. My lips parted. He accepted the invitation, slanting his mouth over mine. Like they always did, my surroundings faded until there was only Damon and what he was doing to me.

His fingers bit into my hips as his mouth moved expertly over mine, awakening me in all the right ways. I arched into him. The slow pressure of his hands as they wandered over my hips then the small of my back made me shiver with need.

He slowed the kiss then pulled back, resting his forehead against mine. His breath crashed into me from the herculean restraint he'd managed. I blinked the world back into focus. The sound of water, people laughing and talking, and that we stood in the water, where everyone could see what we were doing, slammed back into focus.

"D!" Phoenix yelled from the small bank of sand.

I shifted in his arms to see what Phoenix wanted. He held a Frisbee.

"Perfect," I said.

"I thought you hated sports."

"I don't consider Frisbee a sport."

Damon chuckled. "All right, hotshot, let's see what you've got."

A small smile curved my lips, and I waded to the right, putting enough distance between us so that when Phoenix threw it, we would have enough room. When I stopped, Phoenix let the orange disk soar. It was a perfect throw, but I'd expected it to be. Damon caught it with ease then lobbed it to me. I snatched it from the air and laughed at the surprise stamped on his gorgeous face. Whipping it from my fingertips, I sent it to Phoenix.

"Aren't you full of surprises?"

I winked at Damon. We played for a half hour until Julie distracted Phoenix. She was on the poms team and an all-around nice person. She was one of the people, like Tucker, who had rolled her eyes at the bullshit I'd been dealt at school and had shown her support by talking to me in the halls or the class we had together.

When Phoenix dropped the Frisbee on his towel and went with Julie to a folding table with Solo cups and drinks, I moved through the water until I was near Damon. He slung an arm around my waist, and I leaned into him.

Bending to my ear, he whispered, "As far as fake dates go, this has been pretty good."

"It has." I was surprised that I meant it.

I rested my head on his shoulder and watched a few people hit a beach ball in the water. Damon maneuvered us into deeper water and slightly away from a group of girls inching closer. After another sweep around the party, I noticed Gia wasn't in attendance. Neither were her two new besties, Tina and Rebecca.

"I noticed too."

I peered up at him. "You're a mind reader now?"

"Nah, I'm just getting to know you better." His hand squeezed my hip reassuringly. "It doesn't matter. We did what we needed to today. People are getting used to seeing us together, but it won't be enough to convince them you're more than a temporary thing. Especially after I took Gia out a few times."

"Wow, I feel so… insignificant."

He bopped my nose, and I wrinkled it.

"I'm just saying that, if you don't end up moving, we need to do this fake dating thing and be seen for a lot longer for people to buy it as real," he explained.

Not a hardship. "And what do you propose we do next?"

He bent and nuzzled my neck, and I barely caught the moan that wanted to escape my lips. The things he did to me.

"I have a fight coming up tonight, and I want you to go with me. After, we can go to a party, or I can take you home."

"I'm not crazy about the Ring. And there will be so many people." That would be the perfect place for nasty girls to ambush me. I wasn't as worried about guys because word had spread quickly among them and the football team that I was off-limits.

"You'll be with me and, when I'm in the Ring, with Phoenix or Shane. I'll make sure they don't leave you alone."

What he said made sense. "Okay." I just hoped I wouldn't regret it.

CHAPTER FIFTEEN

SKYLAR

#CatchingFeelings

"You're dating this boy?" Mom's voice was almost a monotone. "Are you sure that's wise?"

How do I explain it without lying? "It's more complicated than that. But yeah, I'm going out with him tonight."

"I trust that you know what you're doing." Mom pressed the power button, and sound filled the family room from the movie channel that had been on last.

I hated lying to her, but I couldn't say much. *I'm dating Damon to get the jerks off my back that Gia sicced on me.* Yeah, no way would I get into that because Mom might confer with Gabriella, and having Gia's parents involved in my nightmare was more than I wanted to handle.

While Mom flipped through channels, I leaned against the door and studied her. Dark circles hung under her eyes, and she wore her favorite pair of leggings and an oversized, threadbare T-shirt.

"Are you okay?" *How have I not realized how exhausted she looks?*

She flashed me a bright smile after settling on a romantic comedy. *Mr. Right* was one of our favorite movies when we needed a laugh and to block out the world. "I'm good, just one of those long days with my most difficult client taking far too much time. And tomorrow, I have another one at the start of the day."

I pushed away from the door and went to sit with her on the couch. "Do you want me to cancel? It's not a big deal. We can have a movie marathon. I'm also due for some *Pitch Perfect* and *Keeping Up with the Joneses*."

Mom laughed. Our favorite part was when Isla Fisher screamed, "My hair!" when she got splashed by a puddle.

She squeezed my hand quickly before releasing it and patting my leg. "I would love that, but you go. I don't think I'll even make it through this first one. Maybe we can do that next week."

"Okay." By the way her eyelids drooped, I knew she was telling the truth about not making it through one full movie. "It's a date." I grinned.

Headlights pierced our front window, swinging through the room in an arc as Damon pulled into the driveway. I got up and said goodbye before heading out. I saw no need for him to come inside.

I shut and locked the door behind me as he exited the SUV. I waved him back in, ignoring his frown as I hurried around the front end of the Range Rover and got into the passenger seat. Energy vibrated off him, making the space feel tense.

"You okay?" I asked.

He hooked his wrist over the steering wheel and turned my way, face granite, blue eyes hard and stormy. I shivered from the intensity. Sometimes, he was almost too much to take in. The sheer power of all that focused energy aimed my way stole my breath.

"What do you want to do after the fight? Party or go back to my house?" he asked.

All right, he wasn't in the mood for questions. And his attitude I was picking up on made me uncomfortable about going to a party. "The Ring should be public enough for tonight. How about we go back to your house? If you're having a party there, just take me home." I wasn't in the mood for more people after the chaos the Ring would be.

He nodded, some of the tension easing from his clenched jaw.

What had set him off? I clicked my seat belt into place, determined to let it go because poking him with more questions wouldn't end well.

I checked my phone. Tucker had texted me earlier, letting me know the location for the night's fight. Not that I needed it, since Damon was driving, but I appreciated it anyway.

I shot off a reply. *Headed there now. You going?*

Tucker: *Not tonight, unless you need backup?*

Me: *Damon is taking me. I should be fine. But thanks.*

I slipped my phone back into my pocket and glanced at Damon's strong profile. I'd promised myself I wouldn't stick my nose in things, but that wasn't my strongest trait. "What happened tonight to make you so"—*what could I say that wouldn't be offensive?*—"angry?" I braced myself for whatever reaction that might evoke.

"It's nothing. I fight tonight. Let it go."

It wasn't nothing, but I would do as he asked—for the time being. I couldn't make any promises after the Ring.

We drove silently for the half hour to the crappy neighborhood where that evening's fight would take place. The closer we got to the abandoned warehouse, the worse our surroundings became. Broken, boarded-up windows of empty storefronts grew more frequent. Old beat-up cars passed us. In Damon's Range Rover, I felt like a moving target and didn't breathe a sigh of relief until he parked in the cracked blacktop parking lot and rounded the vehicle to open my door. That time, I was more than happy to let him escort me.

It was early yet, but plenty of cars filled the lot. Damon's large hand enveloped mine, and a strange sense of safety quelled my unease over the neighborhood. We cut through the crowd already forming a line to get in from the academy and whatever other school the fighters were from. I braced myself for outrage, but the bouncer waved us through.

I wasn't sure why I thought anyone would say something. I was with Damon. It was weird to get used to how the world bent over backward for him, and the part of me that used to find it annoying had died a fast death without me even realizing it.

It had to be because of everything he was doing to help me while staying within the imaginary lines I'd drawn in the sand against fighting back and hurting Gia. I knew it went against his instincts, but for me, he'd relented. I couldn't overlook that. He wasn't such a bad guy.

The crowd inside was oppressive and teeming with excitement for the pending violence. It felt hungry, and an involuntary shiver racked my body. Damon glanced over his shoulder, a question in his eyes. He must've felt it through our linked hands as he pulled me toward the middle of the ground floor and a makeshift ring that had been set up for the fights.

I shook my head, indicating it was nothing. His brows furrowed. I knew he didn't believe me, but he didn't stop and push to find out why. A roar rippled through the densely packed place as a right hook caught one of the guys in the Ring at just the right place. He stumbled back, going down to one knee.

The closer we got, the faster my pulse hammered against the skin. Damon stopped and pulled me to him. Wrapping an arm around me, he held me against his side, sheltering me from the violent energy, even temporarily.

"Are you okay?"

"Yeah," I lied. "The crowd seems hungrier than normal."

A slow, wicked grin spread across his mouth before his low chuckle caused the hairs on the back of my neck to rise. "One kid just got out of juvie and is back at the public high school not far from here."

My eyes widened, and a stab of fear hit me. "Don't tell me you're going up against him." *Please don't.*

"Okay."

Fuck. He was. I wound my arm around his waist and momentarily reassured myself that he was fine. He could handle it.

"Hey." Two fingers under my chin, and he tipped my head up so our eyes met. "What's goin' on? You're not worried about me, are you?"

"Pff." I pushed out a burst of air then rolled my eyes. "Please. Would I worry about the godlike Damon Savage?"

Something I couldn't decipher sparked across his features, easing the harshness he'd worn since he'd picked me up. "Good. I couldn't imagine the only girl in school who hates me catching feelings."

"Only in your wildest delusions would that happen."

His rich laughter danced along my skin just as Phoenix, Shane, and Tracey joined our group of two. I was almost sad that they'd arrived. But that meant their matches were close to starting, and I was closer to getting out of that place. Gia might think the Ring was exciting, but I didn't.

"Sky." Phoenix grinned. "Ready to see our boy kick some ass?"

I pursed my lips but nodded. I saw no reason to get into everything I didn't like about the scene. It would only make him laugh.

"I see you." Phoenix winked.

Damon shot his cousin a look as Shane said hi. Tracey didn't bother, and when a few of her friends showed up, she turned her back on Damon and me to talk with them, her hand still entwined with Shane's.

As the guys tired on the center mats, Phoenix helped tape Damon's hands. That told me he would be going next. I hoped we would leave after. I didn't like the energy in the crowd.

The announcer called the fight when one of the guys didn't get up. I hadn't bothered to look too closely to see if I knew either of them. As the fighters were helped out of the Ring, a heavy silence swept through the space, and I looked in the direction several people were looking.

The crowd parted, and what looked like a hardened criminal who might have been held back a few years headed for the Ring.

I gasped. "Is that who you're fighting?"

I'd whispered, but it didn't matter. My question drew the cold, dead gaze of the other fighter. His eyes lingered on me before moving to Damon. Damon released me instantly and stepped forward while seamlessly nudging me behind him. Phoenix mirrored his move, standing shoulder to shoulder with his cousin. Shane did something similar, and I stood with Tracey behind the wall they presented. For once, she didn't have a nasty comment. She looked just as concerned as I was by the monster climbing into the Ring.

Damon pulled off his shirt and handed that, along with his wallet, phone, and keys, behind him to me. I grabbed them and held on tight, wishing I could do the same to him rather than his things. Then he moved away, and Phoenix shifted into his space, blocking me again.

What did all that even mean? I wasn't Damon's girlfriend. Not really. *Do they know something about that guy that I don't?* Whatever it was, it couldn't be good.

The announcer did his thing, and only then did Phoenix and Shane relax their stances enough for Tracey and me to move around to their sides so we could watch the fight. The guys circled each other, pure menace and concentration etched into their features.

Damon moved fast with a powerful right hook. I hadn't even realized he planned to move. He gave no tells. The punch landed, and Mitch, the monster, stumbled back a half step from the impact.

I curled my hand around Phoenix's arm as the two beasts circled each other, launching combination strikes, kicks, and grappling moves that had to be Krav Maga or jujitsu. I wasn't familiar with either, but Tucker would be. I wished he were there to explain some of it to me—anything to lessen the fear slowly closing my throat and my ability to breathe normally.

A brutal hit opened a cut above Damon's eye. But Mitch wasn't much better with his split lip and one eye almost swollen shut.

Phoenix bent to speak directly in my ear. "He'll be fine. Look at the way he's calculating Mitch's movements. Damon knows what he's doing."

I paid closer attention. Damon was faster. He moved in and out of reach, delivering more frequent hits than Mitch managed. As I tried to erase my irrational fear and succeeded minutely, I noticed even more. Damon seemed to sense when Mitch would go for a right hook, and he pivoted just enough for the shot to miss. I saw the way he hadn't tired, though his opponent, while still dangerous, was slowing just a little. Damon seemed to draw on so many details that made his opponent's attempted hits a little less effective, or an outright miss. I hadn't realized it before.

When an opening presented itself, Damon went into beast mode and took advantage, raining punches fueled by cold fury on the other guy.

The crowd went crazy, and I felt their push at my back. Shane moved Tracey in front of him and helped block for me, giving us space so we weren't jostled. I sensed the unrest around us. Pockets of the crowd seemed to want blood. It bordered on something dark and ominous just waiting to erupt.

I refocused on the fight as it wound down some. They'd already been in there for longer than I thought possible. But Damon was a machine, and the guy he fought wasn't far off.

I glanced down when Damon took a nasty kidney punch and noticed the red marks my nails had left on Phoenix's skin. I tore my hand off him, and he shot me a wink. He hadn't said anything. It made me pause for half a second about how he looked out for me. Not only that, but I appreciated how he'd taught me to watch the fight and what was happening more than anything.

Why did I think the Elite sucked? It was confusing. Part of me still hated them. They were assholes. But then they did things like what Phoenix had and flipped the switch on my prior assessment.

The jury was still out. I refused to let them get too close. I couldn't because, eventually, Gia would come around and realize what she'd done. And I would forgive her. She deserved that after helping me when I needed it most.

My skin prickled, and I tore my gaze from Damon and Mitch as they traded punches to search for its source. Not ten feet from where I stood, a pair of brown eyes bore into mine with so much animosity that I almost stepped back. Gia was there, and she'd seen more than I'd realized.

It wasn't long before the fight was called in Damon's favor. When he stepped off the mat, his opponent melted into the crowd in the opposite direction. Only then did I take my first full breath. Then I was in Damon's arms, and his lips crashed down on mine.

The way he kissed me was wild—untamed. He devoured my

mouth, sending jolts of desire through my heated body as I returned the kiss just as fiercely. I moaned, and he swallowed it, pulling me impossibly closer. Someone bumped into me, and a sliver of reality returned.

He must have felt the impact because he broke the kiss, menace rolling over his taut features as he sought who was responsible.

"Sorry, Sky." Shane cringed. "I was stretching."

I relaxed in Damon's arms, patting his shoulder when he growled at his cousin. "It's fine."

I pushed on Damon's chest until he loosened his hold. I would feel better if we were both aware of our surroundings. He must have come to the same conclusion, since he grimaced, and after holding up his hand to one of the guys at the corner of the Ring, they tossed a small white towel to him. He pressed it against the still-bleeding cut over his eye.

"Do you want to go get that looked at?"

"No. It's nothing. I want to stay for Shane's and Phoenix's matches."

Damon removed the towel from his cut. The bleeding had stopped. He kept the cloth balled in one hand, wrapping his other arm around my shoulders and pulling me into him. We watched the next few fights while he and Shane or Phoenix shouted encouragement, depending on who was in the Ring.

When they were done, we got the hell out of there. Damon seemed as eager as I was to put the Ring behind us.

"Mitch, the guy I fought, looked at you in a way I didn't like."

"Yeah, I got that. Thanks for the human shield."

His lips twitched at the corners, but he resisted the smile. "I worried he might stick around."

"Oh." That was why he came to me in a hurry once his fight was done. "He won't go to the academy, right?"

"No. If the fight hadn't turned out the way it did, then

maybe. But it was even enough that he shouldn't feel the need for revenge."

"Yeah, I don't get why you do that. It only takes one time for you to get busted, then what happens to your future? Or if a guy like that flips out outside the Ring, when you're not expecting it?"

Damon pulled into his long driveway and up to his even bigger house within the gated community. "You worry too much."

"And you don't worry enough." The house was dark except for the front entrance light and one or two on the first floor. "Are your dad and stepmom home?"

"No." A wicked grin curved his firm mouth.

My stomach fluttered. We would be alone inside his giant house. I could have wondered why he wanted me to come over, but that would be stupid. I knew, and I wanted it too. That kiss had branded me. I needed more.

I opened my mouth, and he shot me an annoyed look. "No more questions."

I snapped my lips together for the time being.

He parked in one of the garages then whisked me inside, through the gourmet kitchen, and up a flight of stairs on the way to his bedroom. Tingles raced over my body. We weren't going fast enough.

We passed a door on the right, then he opened his, farther down the hall on the left. He flicked on the light, and I swept my gaze around the masculine room.

"I'll just be a minute." He went through another door that had to be the bathroom.

The sound of running water told me he was showering. Good. I didn't want any of that other guy's bodily fluids on me.

While I waited, I trailed my fingers over the top of his desk, where a framed picture sat of the Savage brothers and their cousins. I picked it up and smiled at how happy they looked on the beach behind the house, a football tucked under Phoenix's arm as they grinned at the camera. Tattoos climbed up their arms and across their chests. One look made it apparent that their bodies were athletically gifted and droolworthy.

The water shut off, and I set down the frame, glancing at the other pictures. One on his dresser was of a dark-haired woman with her arms around two young boys. It had to be their mother. I wanted to study it closer, but the door opened, and I quickly moved away.

Damon emerged, steam wafting after him and a towel wrapped around his hips. A drop of water rolled down his chest, and I inched closer, watching its path until I was close enough to trace the trail it had made.

He sucked in a breath as I followed the path with my fingers down his abs, and I glanced up. His pupils eclipsed almost all of the blue in his eyes, and I froze at the raw hunger within them. Then he cupped the back of my neck and slowly lowered his mouth to mine. One touch, and the banked desire between us ignited.

A slight pressure from his fingers, and he tilted my head for a better angle to deepen the kiss. I moaned, and he swallowed the sound. The caress at the hem of my shirt had me squirming against him. I couldn't get close enough.

He broke the kiss long enough to pull my shirt over my head. I flicked open my bra, and he helped me out of it. The rest of my clothes landed in a pile at my feet. He looked his fill as I stood before him. I didn't care that the light was on. I was so turned on I would have done anything. My skin felt uncomfortably tight. I needed his hands on me, and a whimper left my mouth.

That was all it took. He stepped closer, palmed my ass, and lifted me into his arms. I wrapped my legs around his waist. Holding onto his shoulders, I wound my arms around his neck and kissed him like it was my last breath.

He wrapped his arms around my back as he walked us to a wall. I gasped at the cool feel of it. Then he was touching me. His open-mouthed kisses traveled from my neck to my shoulder. Burying my hands in his hair, I gave in to how he made me feel. Every nerve ending was on fire. He played me like an instrument, knowing how and where to touch me to drive me wild.

"Damon," I begged. "Please."

My core throbbed. I wanted him inside me. He leaned against me, holding me in place as he contorted to reach a drawer in the nightstand beside his bed. Through the haze of my lust, I heard the crinkle of a condom wrapper, then he was pressing against my entrance. A wanton moan escaped my lips, ending with a gasp as he pushed inside me. I arched with the delicious way he filled me.

His grip tightened on my ass as he plunged in and out, going impossibly deep. When his hand dipped between our bodies and brushed against my swollen clit, I tightened around him. A slight pressure and two pumps, and I exploded.

The room spun as he pulled me from the wall and onto the bed. My back hit the mattress, and he was moving, pounding into me. His biceps flexed as he held himself over me, and I drank in every dip and bulge of his magnificent body, my fingers greedily following my hungry gaze.

Sensations built, and I met his powerful movements with an insatiable need. He slid a hand under the small of my back and lifted me, changing the angle of his thrust, and stars burst behind my eyes. I screamed his name as I came. It didn't take him long to chase my orgasm with his own.

His large, heavy body collapsed on top of mine, and I welcomed his weight for as long as I could stand it. But breathing was a necessity, so I poked him in the side. He laughed, smiling down at me.

"Too heavy?" He rolled onto his side, grabbed a Kleenex

from the nightstand, and disposed of the condom, tossing it into a garbage can by his desk. Then he dragged me close so I was partially lying on his chest, my legs tangled with his.

We lay there in silence for a few minutes, each lost in our thoughts. Eventually, I needed to get up to use the bathroom. I didn't want to leave the small cocoon we'd created, but I didn't have much choice. I excused myself, grabbing my panties and shirt on the way.

Afterward, I rejoined him on the bed, where he rested his back against the headboard, his long, muscular legs stretched out and crossed at the ankles. He'd grabbed a pair of gray sweats and put them on but had forgone the shirt. I wouldn't complain. I sat cross-legged on his big bed. I should have gone home, but I wasn't ready. He must have felt the same way because he made no move to get up.

"You were impressed. Come on." His grin was pure mischief. "You can tell me."

I wouldn't pad his ego. He wasn't hurting in the confidence department. "You were okay. Fierce for sure, but you could improve in some areas." I almost ruined it by laughing when shock widened his eyes.

"And what areas might those be?"

His quiet words made me shiver from the sense that I'd faced off with a panther waiting to strike. "You wobbled a few times when that huge guy tried to take you down. I bet if you did yoga, you could fix the problem."

"Yoga?" His brows furrowed, a speculative gleam flashing in his eyes. "That's how you're so toned. I wondered what you did, since you claim to hate sports."

I rolled my eyes. "I run occasionally too."

"Want to run with me sometime?"

"Ah, no. Let me amend that. I infrequently jog."

His shoulders shook from barely restrained laughter. "Okay, so yoga. Want to teach me?"

I grinned. "Sure. Sometime." Doing yoga with him would be an experience, but I was quickly getting ready for round two. I would be late for curfew, but I didn't care.

The way his gaze crawled over my legs, heating my skin everywhere they touched, I knew he was of the same mindset. I uncrossed my legs and crawled toward him on my knees. When I got close enough, he lifted me so I straddled him. It only took one touch, and he had me falling into a haze of desire from which I had no will to escape.

CHAPTER SIXTEEN

DAMON

#GamePlay

Practice Wednesday was brutal, but I loved every minute of it. We did drills until we almost puked. Jackson did throw up. Our next game would be against Mammoth, another academy school with several talented players. It was one of the schools that challenged us to work harder, be better. Coach had us scrimmage, mimicking the offensive and defensive style of the opposing team to get an idea of how best to handle them.

We went to war on the practice field, pushing one another to hit harder, run faster, and anticipate better until we were mentally and physically exhausted. Then we broke into special teams. Shane, Phoenix, and I practiced connecting on the field, executing passes and catches over and over until we did each play without thought. It was hard work, but it would make a difference come game day.

I stood to the right, waiting my turn as Phoenix's elbow went back. He launched the ball to Shane, who'd sprinted down the field and turned a sharp right. The ball dropped magically into Shane's hands, and he ran it into the end zone.

Coach barked out a route, and I took off. When I was at the right spot and looked up, the ball appeared. I snatched it out of the air and ran it in, just as Shane had.

The entire time, I felt Sky's gaze. I wasn't foolish enough to believe she only watched me out there, but it was a nice thought. We ran routes at least twenty more times until Coach called it a day.

As we moved slowly off the field, Phoenix slapped me on the back, and I laughed.

"Not bad today," I said. "We'll be ready for whatever Mammoth has to throw at us."

"You know it." He laughed. "I'm hitting the showers and taking off. Shane and I have dinner with Grandad tonight. He's stoked about the upcoming game."

"All right. Talk to you later." He and Shane went toward the locker room, but I hung back. Helmet off and dangling from my fingers, I climbed the three steps to straddle the bleacher next to Sky.

Her clear blue eyes met mine, and she blew a soft whistle through her full lips. "That was some practice."

"Yeah." I cracked my neck. "I'm going to feel it for a while. We'll be ready for the game, though. Mammoth is no joke, and Coach does a great job of preparing us."

She nodded, and some of her long, dark hair fell over her shoulder.

I wanted to tuck it behind her ear but refrained. "Why did you watch? Is this another one of those articles that I'll have to hunt you down about?"

Her lips curved into a mischievous smile. "Just seeing if there's anything to document." She shrugged. "Call it information gathering."

"No slander? I'm surprised." A warm breeze tore through the stands, drying and cooling my overheated body. I needed to get a shower and food, but she was a temptation I couldn't resist.

"I was hoping you'd have another butterfingers moment." She laughed. "That was the best."

"For you, maybe. I wasn't thrilled about it." But I did like the way her eyes sparkled when she was amused.

"From what I saw on the field today, you have nothing to worry about." A hint of pink stained her cheeks. "But don't let that go to your head. Your ego's already too big to fit through normal-sized doorways."

"Original." I snorted at her cliché comment.

Her smile widened. "I try. Can't win them all."

The need to touch her was intense, and the odd moment of truce between us made it even harder to resist the urge. "Want to get out of here?" My stomach growled. "Grab something to eat?"

She pursed her lips. "I'm not sure that's a good idea."

It probably wasn't. Better to keep our dates in the public eye, since that was the reason for them.

"Fine." I swiped a hand over my face. "There's gonna be a bonfire later tonight. I'll pick you up for it."

Her teeth sank into her bottom lip before she nodded.

I was exhausted, and she seemed content, or maybe tired too. Pushing things by going out to eat alone might not be the best option, so I'd retreated then pivoted tactics. She was worth the wait, regardless of how difficult that could be. But I knew how to play the game, and Sky made me want to more than anyone ever had.

CHAPTER SEVENTEEN

DAMON

#TooReal

Stars twinkled overhead as Sky and I walked through the sifting sand on the beach behind my house Wednesday night. After how well our fake dates had gone, I was more than ready for the next one.

I'd picked her up before her mom got off work, and we'd stayed in her room just long enough to take the edge off how badly I needed her, then it was time to do something together—publicly.

It was the perfect night for a bonfire, which my cousins had readily agreed to when I'd brought it up earlier in the day. I needed another excuse to fake date Sky around our classmates. At school, our actions throughout the day had been consistent. People had backed off of giving her a hard time, and if they didn't, a word here and there brought a swift end to it.

Flames curled and licked the inky darkness, keeping it at bay and highlighting the mob of people farther down the beach and to the right. A few trickled by a distance away, barely out of reach of the light cast by the bonfire.

That was where I stopped, dropping the cooler in the sand. It gave us enough light to see each other but also privacy.

I set up the beach chairs brought from the garage, motioning for Sky to take a seat as soon as I had hers ready. The air held a bite, but we wore jeans and long-sleeved shirts. A storm was supposed to arrive sometime around two in the morning. Since it was midweek, we would have the beach cleaned up long before then.

"Want to go for a walk?" I wasn't ready to sit yet or mix with the rest of the people who'd come.

"Sure." She dropped her sweatshirt over the back of a chair then took my hand when I offered it.

I needed to shake the weird mood I'd been in ever since Dad and Raelyn told me they would be out of town for the weekend. I loved Riley and was glad she was part of the family, but it hadn't been that long since my world had gotten flipped upside down. Everything had imploded the weekend Mom had overdosed on pills. I still couldn't shake the image of her sightless eyes, finally devoid of the pain our dad had caused her by his cheating.

I'd thought the root of the problem was Mom's depression, that it had caused a rift between them. It had been a rude fucking shock to learn that most of her darkest times had been caused by him stepping out on her. It had taught me that I never wanted to be like him—and had dashed my plans to join the empire he'd built, after my NFL career or maybe even instead of it.

Plans changed. I would figure mine out when I did.

"What's the deal with Shane and Tracey?" Sky asked.

I happily deserted my train of thought to delve into my cousin's mess. "What do you mean? They've been dating for a long time."

"Yeah, but Phoenix hates her, and I don't feel like you hold her in high esteem either."

The sand was packed beneath our bare feet, the froth from the breaking waves just out of reach. "Phoenix, and I don't like her because of what she represents. She cares more about Shane's potential future and what that'll mean for her than she cares about him."

"Do you know that for sure? I get it. She's not a warm, fuzzy person, but maybe there's more to their relationship."

"I'm sure there is." I didn't want to reveal any of Shane's secrets. They weren't mine to share.

"Phoenix hasn't had a serious girlfriend, has he?"

"Why are you interested?" Jealousy grabbed me by the throat, and I barely got the question out. *What the hell is that about?* I'd never cared if Jessica or any other girl I banged showed the slightest interest in anyone else.

The full moon caught the flash of her white teeth when she smiled. "Not like that. I'm just curious. He seems so driven."

"In football, yeah."

"Not school?"

"He's fine with school, but football is his life. It's the same with my brother, though Riley rivals that. I think, if given a choice, he would pick her every time." It was weird, but I was okay with that. "She's got diving, so she's the perfect fit for him. They both have the same work ethic."

"She's pretty incredible. I wanted to hate her when I had to interview her, and I was prepared to watch a semi-good diving competition. But holy shit, that girl is a prodigy. Short of the Olympics, I've never seen anything like it."

"You watch the Olympics?" I couldn't picture it. Presidential debates and any other current events seemed more of a fit for her.

"I like skiing, and Mom likes diving. She went crazy when she heard about Riley's dive."

"Your mom is pretty cool."

"She is." The affection in her voice was palpable.

I rubbed my chest, trying to chase away the ache.

"It's been the two of us for so long. We have movie nights when she isn't too tired from the crazy-long hours she works."

"She does hair, right?"

"Yeah. She saved Gia from that nightmare DIY-hair job."

We walked a few more feet, her much smaller hand warm in mine.

"It kills me that she knows what's happening, or part of it, between Gia and me. The only good thing is that I could talk to her and she hasn't told Gabriella."

"Who's that?"

"Gia's mom. She's almost like a second mom to me. She would be heartbroken, and Gia's dad would force us to sit in the same room until things were resolved."

"Maybe she should tell Gabriella, then."

"No."

I let it go. It still bothered me, though. I would have to revisit that topic later. "Did you and Tucker ever date?"

She punched my arm. "No. He's a good friend, and what you did to him was bullshit. I hope you apologized."

I said nothing. I would do it again. I didn't like another guy putting his arm around her.

"I mean it, Damon. He's my friend. You owe him an apology."

"He wants to get in your pants."

"Careful. It's beginning to sound like you care."

I huffed. I wouldn't go there. I stepped over a mound of shells that the ocean had dumped on the shoreline or some kid had dragged from the ocean's floor. Sky's grip tightened in mine as she avoided the sharp shells.

"Not that it's your business, but Tucker's never liked me that way. If he did, he has enough confidence that he would have asked me out. So when I say he's a friend and only a friend, you need to believe me. Bullshit guy radar or not."

I laughed. "You're cute when you think you get guys." I

turned us around, and we headed back toward the chairs, avoiding heavy or personal topics. Instead, we compared music likes and dislikes and concerts we'd attended or planned to see.

When we returned to our beach chairs, I handed her a drink from the cooler. I took my one and only, since I would have to drive her home in a few hours. Even though it went against what I wanted, I planned to hang out and talk with her without demanding something in return.

We sat in comfortable silence until I broke it with a tricky question. "Have things improved between you and Gia?"

I felt rather than saw Sky deflate. If I thought about it, I could probably relate. I would feel the same way if something came between my brother or cousins and me. Then again, I didn't see that ever happening. We were tight and had been since we were little. An uneasy part of me whispered, *Wasn't that what Sky and Gia were?*

But they weren't bonded by family. *It's not the same.*

"Gia can hold a grudge better than anyone I know. She's hurt and angry and blames me for screwing things up with you. So no, things aren't better."

"I'm sorry, Sky."

She shifted to look at me rather than the fire. "Why? You didn't do anything."

"I was an equal part in the deception." More precisely, I'd blackmailed Sky and enjoyed every minute of it.

She shrugged. "It is what it is."

I didn't like the melancholy tone I'd set and needed to change that fast. "I've been reading your articles about the home games."

"Oh?"

I clamped down, barely suppressing my laughter. "They're illuminating."

"Do tell." Her tone was dry, but the corners of her mouth twitched, telling me she liked how I teased her.

"They're not as scathing as they used to be. You're warming up to me. Dare I say you like me?"

She smacked my shoulder. "I write unbiased truth, as any good reporter should."

"Yeah, I don't think so. That article at the start of the year says otherwise."

"Please." She rolled her eyes. "I told it like I saw it. You sucked in that practice."

"Maybe it was because a smokin' hot blue-eyed harpy distracted me."

She laughed. "Whoa, you better reword that harpy business."

"In the beginning, we clashed pretty well, and you use your words like weapons."

"Fair enough. But take note, that didn't win you any points."

"Got it. I'll call you a goddess instead. Better?"

Her grin filled with mirth. "Now you're talking."

"Are you gonna admit it?"

"What?"

"That you enjoy football now," I pressed. "It's obvious in the turn your articles have taken that your bias against athletes is lifting."

She tilted her head, intelligent eyes seeing more than I wanted her to. "Are you fishing for compliments?"

Maybe. "No. I just wanted to point out how much you like football. You're a closet fan."

"Please. Let's not get ahead of ourselves here." She pursed her lips. "Fine. I see why people like the game."

"And?"

She rolled her eyes. "And not all athletes are ass-letes. But my judgment with you remains undecided."

"I'll take it." It was a huge shift since we'd faced off at the barbeque at the end of summer. "But I think your viewpoint changed somewhat when you and Riley hit it off last year."

"Yeah. She's pretty cool. I'm glad we've become friends," she agreed.

"She and my brother will be at the game this weekend. I'm sure she would want you to sit with them."

"I'll do that." She picked at the hem of her shirt. "What are the college-level classes you're taking?"

I pushed out a breath. It was a heavier conversation than I'd expected to get into. "Business, mostly."

"You want to major in business? I thought you said you were going into corporate law."

"I wanted to be a lawyer, like my dad. I planned to study business and law to join his company someday."

"You say that like you don't want to anymore."

I listened to the waves crashing against the shoreline interspersed by the music pumping out of a portable speaker and the murmur of conversations not too far from our little bubble of privacy. It didn't take long for me to decide to show her the darkness inside me. I had a feeling it matched what was in her to some degree.

"That part of my plan ended when my mom passed. I haven't seen eye to eye with my father after that day."

"I'm sorry. That sucks. But if it's what you love, you can still pursue it. You don't have to work with him."

That was another thing I had wrestled with. "Right. I don't have to make any decisions yet. I want to get to Thane and play ball with my brother and cousins. That will all work out eventually."

We fell back into silence, and the sounds of the beach party grew. Eventually, we would join my cousins and hang out until it was time to take her home. I just wanted a little more time with Sky all to myself. The more I was around her, the more I wanted what we had on our fake dates to be real because it had already become real for me.

CHAPTER EIGHTEEN

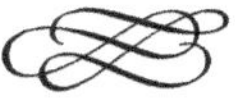

SKYLAR

#BossBitch

With my bag over my shoulder, I used the beach access where Damon said he was setting up for his first yoga lesson behind his house. I couldn't wipe the smile off my face if I tried. It'd been a permanent fixture since he'd called after football practice to admit he'd thought more about my advice and wanted to try adding yoga into his routine.

Just after lunch, the sun was directly overhead. It was a gorgeous day, perfect for yoga on the beach. A slight breeze teased the wispy hair that hadn't made it into the messy bun on my head. As I cleared the house, a vast expanse of sand and blue water that sparkled like diamonds from the sun's rays greeted me. I loved the beach. Mom and I both adored it. When we had time over the summer, we enjoyed a day there with a bag of books, an umbrella, and a cooler packed with snacks and drinks.

Then I saw him. He wasn't wearing a shirt. Tingles attacked me, and my breath quickened at the image he presented in his gray-and-white board shorts.

Like a sun god, his bronze skin beckoned me to touch it. Impossibly broad shoulders, stacked muscles that tapered to a trim waist, and those abs—I wanted to trace each one then follow with my tongue.

He bent and positioned one of the beach yoga mats on the sand, his biceps flexing with every movement. A wave of dizziness swept over me, my core heating to an uncomfortable temperature. I squeezed my thighs together against the ache from watching him.

But that wasn't why I was there. *Yoga.* I huffed, kicking off my flip-flops. In black bike shorts and a matching sports bra, I was ready. My bag held my bikini, a bottle of sunscreen, water, and a cover-up. And a book. I snorted at the ridiculousness of going anywhere without one—especially the beach.

The mats in place, Damon straightened. A grin curved across his mouth, and he shoved his dark hair out of his face. My stomach flipped at how gorgeous he was. I bent and retrieved my flip-flops, giving myself a second to wipe the longing from my expression.

"Hey." I crossed the sand quickly, since it was hot from the sun, purposely stopping on the other side of the thickly woven mats, away from him. "Ready for your first lesson?"

Slowly, his gaze traveled from my head to my toes then back again. "Lookin' hot, Sky. Sure you want to do yoga?" His grin shifted into a wicked smirk. "I can think of something better to do."

"Yes, hotshot." I laughed when he grunted. "Come on, let's get started."

I set my bag on the sand and dropped my flip-flops next to it before stepping onto the yoga blanket. Its colors were beautiful —a black-red-and-orange diamond in the center surrounded by blue, followed by different-colored stripes on both ends.

"Did you buy these for today?" If he had, I wanted to know

where he'd gotten them. Mom and I had a set, but they weren't as lovely.

"No." He mimicked the way I moved to my hands and knees. "Louisa, our housekeeper, worked a half day this morning, and once I got home, I asked her if we had any. I guess we have a bunch of them tucked in the back of the towel closet. I had no idea."

"Does your dad or Raelyn do yoga?"

"Not that I know of. They're out of the house until tonight, which is convenient."

I ignored his subtle invitation. We were doing yoga. I glanced at his position. Like me, he'd placed his hands beneath his shoulders, lining up his knees beneath his hips.

"I'm sure you've heard of this one. It's downward-facing dog, and it works several things, one of them being a fantastic stretch for hamstrings and calves. We'll straighten our legs, pushing through our hands to lift our hips."

I pushed up and held the pose then twisted my head to see how he was doing. "Push your heels down to shift the weight off your arms." I waited for him to do as I said. "Good. Spread your fingers."

It was a fairly easy pose, but the stretch was killer if a person wasn't used to it. Since he stretched regularly in football, he had no problem establishing the correct pose.

After we'd held the pose for about a minute, I brought him out of it by bending the knees. "The next one is warrior pose. It strengthens the quadriceps and arms and helps with balance."

I gave easy instructions, taking him through warrior poses one and two, holding the second for a minute until we switched legs and repeated the exercise.

With each pose, I regained my inner balance and could mostly ignore how his presence affected me. We moved seamlessly through the equestrian pose, the plank, then had some trouble with the one-legged pigeon. When he tried to copy me for the king portion of it, my lips twitched. I pressed them together to stop myself from smiling at his low grunt and his back leg that he could not get off the mat.

"Your lower back is stiff. It's okay to skip this one. You'll get there. We'll try the extended pose. Slide your knee forward and between your hands, then move your foot over and walk your hands forward."

"You're killing me." He hunched over his front leg, the back one extended, and held the correct form.

I chuckled softly. "It's a stretch. The more you do it, the better you'll get. Your muscles are tight. Wait until we go through the butterfly and standing forward bend."

He shot me a side-eye as we shifted to the cobra serpent pose. "What kind of hell are you putting me through?"

I giggled and had to work hard to maintain the correct form. "I promise it'll help if you keep doing this short set a few times weekly." *But would he?* "Maybe we should bet on it. You know, if you'll keep doing it or not?"

After I took him through the harder stretches I'd warned him about, we settled into the wide-angled, seated forward bend, during which his eyes flashed retribution, and I dissolved into laughter.

"I'll take the bet that you won't stay with this yoga routine three times a week."

His lips peeled back in a snarl as a bead of sweat ran down his temple to his cheek. "You're on."

"You have to prove it," I challenged. "I want video evidence. Set up your phone and record it. I expect three a week for the next month."

"What do you want if you win?"

I took a second to think about it, shifting on the soft blanket that worked incredibly well for yoga. "These mats. If I win, then I get to keep them." It sounded like they'd gone unused for years, and Damon said his family had many. *Would they miss two?* Somehow I doubted it, which was the only reason I was comfortable enough to bet something like that.

"Deal." He held my gaze, and a slow smirk that I didn't like made his features dangerous in a flash. "And if I win?"

"I don't know. You feel good about yourself?" I suggested.

Lust dilated his eyes, and I sucked in a breath at how fast his expression changed.

"I get to fuck your sweet little ass," he proposed.

My mouth fell open, and I choked on spit when I inhaled. I coughed and sputtered. Only after Damon reached over, grabbed water from a small cooler near the end of his blanket, and casually handed it to me did I finally get ahold of myself.

"Ah, no." My body tensed, and a jolt of adrenaline raced through me. "That's a strict no-entry zone."

"That's the bet. You already agreed, and there's no backing out."

I narrowed my eyes, calculating his schedule and if he would do the thirty-minute yoga poses several times a week. If he missed sending me a video even one time, I would win. "Fine."

I had it in the bag. He'd groaned like a baby during several stretches, unable to hold the attempted pose for longer than a few seconds.

I wanted to push him over with how sure he looked. I guided him into the half lord of the fishes pose to finish our session.

When we were done, we downed some water. I had no idea what we were doing past yoga. *What is this? And why did he tell me to bring a bathing suit?* I sat cross-legged while he stretched out on his back, arms crossed behind his head.

"I should get going," I said.

He pushed onto his elbows and turned his head so our eyes met and held. "Why? It's the perfect day for a fake date."

I sipped water as my mind whirled with how bad of an idea that would be. The more I hung out with him, the more I liked it. And what we were doing had an expiration date—in about a week if my mother's plan to move actually happened. "No one from school is around, so it hardly counts."

"Go change, and we'll walk down the beach. I promise you we'll run into people."

"Okay." I stood, shook out my blanket while he did the same, then handed it to him. Grabbing my stuff, I followed him to the back wrought iron gate surrounding his family's pool and backyard.

He punched in a code, and the door swung open. After I followed him, he shut it and took my hand in his. I didn't think about the gesture too much. The more we hung out or pretended in front of others, the more automatic his small touches had become.

My gaze bounced around the Savages' luxurious pool with its grotto and waterfall and sun shelf, complete with lounge chairs and built-in sun visors, their hot tub off to one side. An outdoor kitchen had a dining area, and two sets of sliding glass doors that I was sure would open like an accordion offered indoor-outdoor living. It was paradise, and a part of me longed to experience it, even for one day.

The kitchen, where we entered his home, was incredible, with miles of marble countertops and an overly large island. Damon showed me to a bathroom on the first floor, where I changed into my bikini. After reapplying sunscreen, I slipped on my cover-up and stuffed my exercise clothes into my beach bag.

When I returned to the kitchen, it was to find Damon leaning against the island, waiting for me.

"Ready?"

"Sure." I hiked my bag higher on my shoulder.

"You can leave that here." He took my bag and set it in the mudroom off the kitchen. "We'll grab it later."

We retraced our steps back on the beach and walked along the firm sand by the shoreline in companionable silence. A few birds flew overhead, and I squinted from the sun's bright rays reflecting off the water. A sense of peace blanketed me as gentle waves broke near our footsteps. Shells were scattered haphazardly, some shifting as the waves rearranged them or carried and deposited new ones.

Damon's fingers were laced with mine, and every once in a while, our arms brushed, sending jolts of awareness into me. It was hard to believe I hadn't been able to stand him at the beginning of the summer. Things were changing. I liked hanging out with him. He was still an asshole. But he had some redeeming qualities I'd never noticed before. Like his loyalty to his brother and cousins and anyone he cared about.

I still held out hope that we wouldn't have to move. When Mom got home at night, she was so exhausted from fitting clients into her two weeks' notice that she hadn't brought it up again or even broached the subject of packing. *And if we don't leave, what will that mean for Damon and me?*

I pressed my lips together, annoyed with myself. It didn't mean anything, no matter how much my feelings had shifted. *This is fake.* I needed to keep reminding myself of that.

Lost in thought, I didn't register the increase in noise right away. A high-pitched shriek pierced my awareness, and I turned toward the sound about twenty feet from where we were. A large group of people filled the beach. It took a second before I recognized where we were.

"Phoenix and Shane are having a party?"

"Not quite." Damon's voice rumbled low. "They invited some people over to play volleyball, but it looks like those people included a bunch more."

I mentally braced myself. It was late afternoon on a Saturday, so things could quickly snowball and turn into an all-nighter. I scanned the faces, and when a voluptuous figure with a sleek blond cut caught my eye, I had to fortify my defenses. Gia and her evil friends were in attendance.

Damon gave my hand a quick squeeze. He must have noticed her too. And not only was she there but Jessica and the rest of the girls who hung around the Elite. *Great. This should be fun.*

"Ready?" Damon glanced at me.

I pursed my lips. *No. Not at all.* I had zero desire to be in the same space as Gia, Tina, and Rebecca. I couldn't care less about Jessica or anyone else, though. But that was the purpose of our fake relationship—so those people would back the hell off from me. "Yep." I was such a liar.

He must've seen it on my face because he chuckled then released my hand, wrapping his arm around my waist and pulling me against his side. "It'll be fine. Promise."

"D!" Phoenix yelled as we neared. His blond head towered over most of the bikini- and board shorts–clad people. "Come help me with the net."

All four of them were tall, which would only work in their favor if they went into the NFL. Or I thought it would. Some aspects of what made an excellent pro footballer eluded me.

Damon stopped, and since his arm was still around my waist, I did too. "I should help my cousin. You'll be all right for a few minutes?"

My gaze combed over everyone present until I spotted Tucker. "Yeah, but you have to promise me you won't pounce on Tucker when I go talk to him." I tilted my chin up and glared.

He slicked his tongue over his top teeth, saying nothing for three seconds. Then a single nod in answer.

I raised my eyebrows and leveled him with an I'm-not-messing-around expression. "I mean it. He's a friend, and you know what we are, right?" *Nothing.* I didn't say it because of the witnesses, but even so, I suspected he needed the reminder just as much as I did.

"Yeah, McCormick. I hear you." He released me and stalked toward his cousin.

I guess he got the subliminal message loud and clear.

Shaking off the odd displeasure from our exchange, I traveled outside the group, fighting the shifting sand beneath my bare feet until I arrived at Tucker's group—a handful of wrestlers and a few football players.

"Sky." Tucker grinned, giving me a brief side hug. "I didn't know you would be here." His gaze shifted to Gia before finding mine again.

"It's fine." My words were soft and for his ears only. "Don't let what's going on between us change your opinion of her, okay?"

Someday, it would blow over, or I would move, as Mom said, and I didn't want my best friend to lose her only real friends. Those fake bitches wouldn't remain once they realized she couldn't elevate their social status to their desired levels. Or that was my take on why they'd formed such a fast frenemy relationship—only sophomores, they probably still had hopes she would break through the Elite's barriers and bring them with her.

Tucker and I chatted with his wrestling buddies, and I felt Gia's disapproving stare the entire time. Deep voices drew my attention, and I stepped slightly outside the safe circle I'd enjoyed with Tucker to watch as Damon, Phoenix, and Shane returned with two poles and a volleyball net. Jackson, one of the football players, followed with a volleyball.

They got to work setting it up, and I remained fixed in place, soaking in every drool-worthy moment of watching Damon's muscles shift and bunch as he buried the base of the poles in the sand.

A shadow fell across me, and I tore my gaze from him only to land on Rebecca's hostile hazel one. Her red lips were a hard slash in her disgusted expression, and I fought to stop myself from taking a step back as Tina joined her in a shoulder-to-shoulder stance. My only saving grace was that Gia hadn't followed them.

"You shouldn't be here." Tina smirked. "You're a joke."

I crossed my arms over my chest. "Wow, that's original. What's next? Will you call me a slut? Tell me I'm ugly?" I rolled my eyes.

Tina's eyes narrowed. "No need for that. Why state the obvious?"

I shook my head, perplexed by their attitude. "I'm not sure what this little confrontation is about. Are you trying to start something with me that will only further ensure that the Elite block you? Because that's where this is headed. Damon and I are a couple. Do you really think he'll be okay with you two treating me like bitches?"

"He'll be back with Gia soon. You're temporary."

"Or, he'll pick someone else." Rebecca glanced in his direction, and a longing look tightened her features before she smoothed them again. "You're not the right person for any of the guys in the Elite."

"And why is that?" I shouldn't indulge them, but I was curious.

"You're not on the cheer squad." Tina's hand found her hip.

"Or an athlete. And you prefer to fade into the background rather than be the center of attention. How long do you think that'll last with one of them?" Rebecca's head tilted to the side, and she studied me. "They need someone like us. Not a book nerd like you."

I laughed. I couldn't help it. "You keep telling yourself all those things, and we'll revisit where you are in a month. 'Kay?" I pivoted on my heel, which worked better in my mind than in reality, since the sand shifted. But I managed to power through and put some distance between us as Damon finished and sought me out.

He materialized by my side, a mischievous spark in his eyes as he glanced over my shoulder. "You school them?"

"Like a boss." I winked, letting all the bullshit around me roll off my shoulders.

He tugged me to where a game of volleyball was starting, and I let him, determined to have a good time and not to let anything bother me. *Because how many more happy memories will I be able to claim?*

CHAPTER NINETEEN

DAMON

#Addicted

Sky's small fist sliced through the air centimeters from my face as I shifted to the side, using her momentum to knock her arm away. As she rotated from the light impact, I used that to hold her so her arm was caught behind her back. I wrapped an arm around her chest and chuckled at her growl of frustration when she couldn't move.

I'd sparred with her for the past half hour, but I could only take so much before I wanted a taste. All the small touches, like watching the way she moved in black yoga pants, were pushing me over the edge.

"You've improved, but it's gonna take time and repetition until the new moves come naturally."

"Then help me so they do," she said.

I dipped my head, dragging my nose along the curve of her neck, inhaling her sweet vanilla-with-a-hint-of-coconut scent. From the moment she got out of her car in the school's parking lot and we descended to the basement to spar together, I couldn't get the need for her out of my mind. My dick had an agenda, too, and I pushed against her sexy ass.

"Hey, now." She craned her neck to look at me. Fire flashed in her deep-blue eyes.

I knew she remembered our bet. It went against everything in me, but I would let her win—that time—by purposely missing a video. We would circle to what I wanted to do to her later.

"We're done for today," I said.

She frowned, and I caught her full bottom lip between my teeth. I nipped at it, following that with a swipe of my tongue to ease the sting. When I drew back, her lips parted, and her pupils eclipsed the blue. That was all it took with us. One touch, and desire flared to uncontrollable levels.

When she shifted, I loosened my hold on her. Free to move, Sky wound her arms around my neck, and I grabbed her ass, lifting her so her legs wrapped around me. Our mouths collided in a hungry kiss, and I buried my hand in her hair, tilting her for a better angle to taste more of her.

We had spent the entire day at the beach on Saturday, and by Monday night, when we met for our sparring session, I still couldn't get her out of my head. The feel of her soft skin, how incredible she smelled, her infectious laughter—her strength. The need to possess her, to make her scream my name, escalated. I hadn't acted on it then. We'd had a goal that day. But not anymore. We'd already sparred—something she'd wanted and I'd fulfilled.

All I could think about was filling her. And by how she responded to my kiss, our goals were aligned.

I tore my lips from hers and unwound her legs as our breaths crashed together. "I want these off." I tugged at the waistband of her tight pants.

Dazed eyes met mine, and I fought to claim her swollen lips in a hungry kiss. I stomped over to where I'd dropped my keys and wallet with effort. A tether connected us, its strength so great I felt as if I'd waded through quicksand with every step away from her.

Her eyes never left mine as her thumbs hooked into the waistband of her pants, and she shimmied them and her panties down her long, toned legs. She kicked off her shoes then stood before me, bare from the waist down and so goddammed beautiful.

Condom retrieved from my wallet, I tore the wrapper with my teeth, shoved my sweats low on my hips, then sheathed myself before stalking back to her. A slow, wicked grin curved her lips. When I reached her, hands on her hips, she jumped up and wrapped her legs around me. I hissed from the heat of her, straining to bury myself deep inside.

I walked us to the wall then lined up at her entrance. Her nails dug into my shoulders as she moved against me, seeking more than the inch I fed into her. A whimper left her lips before I thrust deep inside. I loved how her head fell back, and she clenched tightly around me.

For a few seconds, I held still, entirely overwhelmed by the sight and feel of her. And before I lost control with my very willing partner, part of me yelled to pay attention to how fucking right everything about it felt.

CHAPTER TWENTY

SKYLAR

#GirlsNight

I sat across from Mom in the ridiculously expensive seafood restaurant that I'd planned as a surprise for her birthday. The midweek reservation had been made the moment I got the job at Chicks-N-Wings, which I'd quit the night of Gia's confrontation and my car's flat tires.

Mom's eyes sparkled, effectively eclipsing her haunted and hollow expression since learning of my dad's pending release from prison. But I wasn't going to think of that. Not that night. My back pressed against the chair and the strap of my purse, which held a wad of cash I would use to pay for our indulgent evening.

"This is such a surprise." Mom clutched the menu between her fingertips, leaning around the edge of it, two spots of pink coloring her cheekbones.

"Happy birthday, Mom." My words were equally soft but filled with love.

"Thanks, honey." She worried her lower lip for a second.

"You know I would have been just as happy with a movie night and popcorn."

I shrugged. "Yeah, I know." She was a no-fuss kind of person, easygoing and generally happy when she wasn't exhausted or freaked out over events that would not be named—and there were a few. "I took that job so we could do this. You deserve to be celebrated."

The server materialized at our table, and I narrowed my eyes at Mom until she laughed then winked. In our short, wordless conversation, she got my message not to order the least expensive thing on the menu. I wanted to spend every last dime stashed in my little black purse on her. She knew me well enough that if she didn't order what she truly wanted, I would do it for her and swap plates.

It was the first time we'd been there, and I wished it wasn't, since the decor was gorgeous, with natural lighting, wood floors, and dark ceiling beams. It offered a rich and decadent feel that put us both at ease.

Mom dropped a bomb after we received our drinks. "I got asked out at work today."

My brows climbed my forehead. "Did you say yes? And what does he look like?"

"He looks like a young Kevin Costner from his *Field of Dreams* movie."

"And you said yes, right?" Mom had a mad crush on that actor.

"Well, not that it matters, since we're moving." She adjusted her silverware, the napkin already on her lap, then took a sip of water. "But I didn't say no."

"Whoa," I leaned forward. "That's progress. So, what happened?"

Her hand smoothed out an imaginary wrinkle on the white linen tablecloth. "I told him that my life was a little... messy right now."

"How did he take it?" My leg bounced under the table as I waited for her answer. "And what does he do for a living?" An important question for so many reasons.

"He was very gracious and made his appointment for a cut in four weeks, even though I told him I might not be in town. But"—the giddy expression she wore while talking about him slipped—"I don't think I'll be here for it."

"You didn't tell me what he does for a living." I redirected the conversation from what could happen. That she'd made the appointment told me all I needed to know. She didn't want to move either. Maybe, just maybe, we could work things out so we didn't have to.

"He's an engineer."

We paused as our salads were delivered.

After a few bites, I circled back. "What kind? Nuclear, chemical, or does he work with structures? I forgot what they're called, environmental engineers?"

"I think the last one. He mentioned something about that house on Fifth Street as a job he just finished."

"Tell me more." I speared lettuce, a blue cheese crumble, and bacon bits onto my fork, pausing halfway to my mouth. "Does he have kids? Never married?"

Mom laughed. "We didn't get into his whole life story. This is the first time I've cut his hair." She took a minute to eat another forkful. "Six years divorced. And he has two boys, one in college and the other working on his master's."

"This is the first guy you've talked about in…" I racked my brain and came up with nothing. "You've never mentioned anyone before."

"Sure I have." Mom ticked off names on the fingers of her left hand. "Kevin Costner, Matt Damon, Idris Elba, and let's not forget Ryan Rey—"

"Those don't count!" I laughed. "Everyday people, that's who I'm talking about. And this guy—what's his name?"

"Liam." She blushed.

"You like him. I think you should give him a chance. Say yes to a date."

Our dinner arrived, the salad plates were removed, and we took a moment to appreciate everything in front of us. God, buttery lobster was my new favorite smell.

"This is amazing, Sky." Mom dabbed at her mouth halfway through her meal. "Thank you."

I wished we could do it more often, but things were too tight for splurging more than once or twice a year. I understood. "You're welcome."

We chatted about everything from her coworkers at the salon to new movies we couldn't wait to watch together when they were released. Dessert came and went, and we finished the evening with cappuccinos. They were placed in front of us with a fancy design in the foam.

"What do you think about light brown or maybe a dark blond for a hair color?"

I tilted my head, trying to picture those shades on Mom. Her hair was the same shade as mine—black. "I guess I could see either one working on you. Why?"

The light that had illuminated Mom's expression since we'd arrived faded, and my spine snapped to attention. *No, please don't.* The night had been perfect. I wanted to shout at her to keep her words in and not let them infect anything.

She toyed with the stem of her wineglass, twirling it between her fingertips. "I'm going to bring home a few boxes of color and some other supplies from the shop so we can change our appearance. Muddy the waters a little to make it harder for Adam to find us."

And like that, the idea of her dating a new guy went up in smoke. That damn ticking clock thundered in my ears, counting down the days until Mom said we had to leave.

My smile wavered. Just as I'd waded into fake dating with Damon, with blinders on to the future, I'd wanted the same for that night—for it to be all about Mom. Luxurious and free from worry. But it seemed we couldn't escape the long-reaching, ominous shadow my dad cast.

CHAPTER TWENTY-ONE

DAMON

#RedZone

I didn't need to look into the stands to know that Sky was sitting with my brother—I could feel her. It was a huge game against a team whose defense was on point. I checked in with my teammates, gauging their readiness as we gathered for a final huddle before the offense took the field after kickoff. Expectation hung in the air, a tangible hunger for the win.

Phoenix checked in with each player, pumping up the team. The way he led us would translate into how we played on the field. His good leadership had cemented a strong sense of trust and loyalty among us. And it showed when we played.

A quick huddle formed, and before my cousin called the play, he shared with the O-line what Shane and I had learned at the cove party, where I'd had my first official fake date with Sky.

"I know some of you haven't secured a spot at Thane or one of the other universities, and you're hungry to do that. Friday night football. It's your game to lay it all out on the field. Scouts are in the audience." Phoenix met each of our gazes. "Let's show them what we're all about."

Energy sizzled around us as our team fed into the line, determined and excited for the game.

"I'm playing to win tonight, which is why Damon will receive first, and Shane and Jackson will be the decoys. Let's get that first touchdown and set the game's tone." Phoenix grabbed the face mask of our offensive guard, Murphy. "Hold the line. Watch for the blitz."

We lined up, and as I waited for the snap, the vision of the play, where I needed to be to catch the ball, solidified. The route didn't matter. My instincts would kick in with how to pivot, who to outrun to get there. I'd studied the film. We'd faced that team before. Anticipating how the defensive tackle, linebacker, and defensive end had played before gave me the map I needed.

The center snapped the ball. Phoenix dropped back, his body language following Shane's route to confuse the defensive line. I spun, breaking through a tackle, then sprinted along the sideline. The defensive end trailed me. My muscles powered to life, toes digging into the grass as I pushed to get where I needed to be. The distance grew between the DE and me. Thirty-yard line, and I angled to the spot where the ball should be. At the red zone, I looked up, and it dropped into my hands like magic.

As I crossed into the end zone, cheers from the crowd erupted. Our fans were on their feet and celebrating. The noise was deafening, and I grinned as I tossed the ball to the referee.

I did no showboating. We were there to do a job—one that we loved. Phoenix, Shane, and I set the tone—my brother, too, when he was a part of the team—and our teammates emulated it.

My teammates slapped me on the helmet and back as we lined up for the two-point conversion. We weren't playing around. We were there for the win.

I could feel the defensive line's fury. They were coming for me, which was what we wanted. Jackson, our tight end, would receive.

When the ball was snapped, the defensive end wrapped me up, and as I went down, Phoenix threw. I shoved the bulky player off me and gained my feet as Jackson caught the ball, securing two extra points.

Our fans went crazy, and still, I didn't search for Sky, no matter how much I wanted to. That game was serious. Not only did I want to impress Thane's coach, but at least three others on the team were looking to get recruited.

Our defense took the field, and I paced along the sideline, willing them to hold the offensive line until we could retake it. We had done what we'd set out to do with that first play—points on the scoreboard. The tone was set, and I was ready to dominate.

CHAPTER TWENTY-TWO

SKYLAR

#Touchdown

The academy's football team was in it to win it. A buzz hummed under my skin from the first play when Damon ran the ball into the end zone. I grinned at Riley, who I sat next to in the stands.

Cole leaned forward on the other side of Riley and pointed at a few men standing on the other side of the goal posts. "That's Thane's scout. You might want to approach him with questions at halftime."

"Good idea." A wave of sadness threatened to disrupt my good mood. I'd told Damon and Phoenix at the cove party that I would write the blog article for the night's game. It would be my last one. Mom still planned on us leaving Monday.

I had one more day to pretend everything was okay. After that, we would pack to leave before my dad was released. I hated every second of it. Damon had become more to me than I'd ever imagined. All the fake dates teetered on the edge of being real, making me want things I couldn't have.

With a glance at the scoreboard to determine we were still in the first quarter, I nudged Riley. I was desperate to maintain the illusion of normalcy. "Didn't Piper go to Thane? Is she making a pest of herself?"

"She's there." Riley shrugged, a wide smile on her mouth. "I don't see her often, and I think my presence bothers her way more than hers does me."

"Is she still chasing after Cole?"

She snorted. "Surprisingly, no. I heard she was dating someone who wasn't an athlete. Maybe premed. I can't remember, but it seems she's focused on school and getting her degree. I've run into her at the library several times and found her with a slew of books open and her head down."

"Huh, I didn't figure that happening. She was so determined to land Cole and be a football wife."

"It's refreshing."

Our gazes snapped back to the field when Phoenix launched the ball to Shane, who plucked it out of the air like they'd practiced the move hundreds of times. We leaped to our feet with the rest of the fans, shrieking and hollering as Shane sprinted down the middle, Montgomery, one of our second-string tight ends, trailing inches behind a pursuing defensive player.

Montgomery launched himself at the defender and wrapped his arms around the guy's waist and took him down, freeing Shane to cross the end zone. Screams pierced my ears from the girls behind me. My heart raced, and I shrieked right along with them. *Who knew football could be so exciting?*

The stands quieted marginally, or enough for us to continue talking. It might have been better if they hadn't.

"This time next year, you'll be at Thane. With Damon." Riley's smirk was knowing.

"Why do you say it like that?" As far as I knew, they were aware that things between us were fake.

"Because"—she leaned close so no one would overhear her—

"I see the way he looks at you. It's the same way your eyes get all dreamy around him. Nothing about your relationship is fake."

"We're excellent actors." I wasn't sure why I refused to acknowledge how I felt, but I'd boarded my denial train and didn't want to jump off it.

"Damon doesn't do things like what he's doing for you. None of them do."

I would regret asking, I knew. "What are you talking about?"

"Cole, Phoenix, Shane, and Damon don't date girls like Damon's dating you as a favor or out of the goodness of their hearts. Damon's invested in you. Nothing about his feelings is casual."

"It doesn't matter even if his feelings were real." I wished things were different. "Damon is the only one who knows this, but I'm moving Monday."

Riley's eyes went flat. "Why?"

I pushed out a breath. I didn't mind her knowing. When we first met, she made it clear that her face couldn't be shown in the blog's article highlighting the meet she was in. It was something we had in common—a threat within the family. And by the way her face shuttered, locking down all emotion, she was well aware of why I had to go. It probably didn't take much for her to surmise, based on our single interaction last year.

"It's not the same as what you faced last year but close enough." I briefly closed my eyes. "Even if something were building between Damon and me, it ends this weekend."

"I'm sorry, Sky." Riley squeezed my hand then released it. "If I can do anything to help, please let me know."

If only. "I had no business going along with Damon's plan once I found out I would be leaving. But I held out hope that Mom would change her mind."

Tension built in the stands, and I redirected my gaze to the field, where our defense tried to contain a play. A collective groan sounded when the opposition's receiver broke through a tackle and managed to stumble into the end zone, football firmly tucked against his chest.

My stomach tight, I scooted to the edge of my seat like the crowd around me. We still had the lead, but I wondered if we could maintain it. I let myself get absorbed into the excitement around me, cheering on our team—at least, it was mine, too, for a little longer.

Every time Damon took the field, I struggled to watch anything else. The way he moved down the field was a thing of beauty. And even though he'd already failed the yoga bet—and I was the new proud owner of his yoga mats—I could swear he'd kept up the routine because how he evaded tackles and pivoted on a dime had an added grace and balance.

I found it highly ironic that I was dating an athlete—even if it was fake—and that I'd enjoyed most of it, including the games. Something inside me was changing. Baseball was still something I refused to entertain, but maybe I'd been wrong to judge all athletes based on my dad.

I didn't want to examine the thought too closely, but I would have plenty of time during the long drive to a destination I had yet to learn from Mom.

I cast another glance at the scoreboard. With four minutes left until halftime, I leaned over to Riley and told her I would head toward the scouts to interview them. People stood or shifted their knees so I could get by. When I got to the stairs, I took a full breath before descending them.

I had no need to hurry, and I enjoyed the slight breeze as it swept a few strands of my hair from my face. The stadium lights would come on toward the end of the game, but there was plenty of light for the moment, and I scanned the bleachers for signs of Gia.

My heart hurt with how things had ended up between us and how I didn't have time to set it to rights—if that was possible.

I paused at the base of the stairs as the other team's quarterback threw a short pass to their tight end. He gained a handful of yards before our defense tackled him.

Our team was on fire, and I was happy for Damon. He'd already secured a spot on Thane's football roster, but it wouldn't hurt to have the scout report back to the head coach about how well he played.

As I made my way along the outskirts of the field, I formulated the questions I wanted to ask. The Elite would get their time in the article, but it was important to share the spotlight with the other players who excelled. And with how Phoenix had done his best to distribute the ball to as many of them as he could, not just Damon and Shane, I would have lots to talk about.

I hurried past our bench before the players left the field. I would've loved to say hi to Damon, but I also needed a clean break. Because crying in front of the entire school would suck, and the way my eyes kept tearing up, it was inevitable.

If I didn't leave before the end of the game, I knew I wouldn't be able to rein in the irresponsible feelings for Damon unfolding in my traitorous heart despite our agreed-upon fake relationship.

It was crazy. Somewhere along the way, he'd come to mean so much more to me than the asshole jock I'd despised. As the whistles, grunts, and crashing of pads vied with the boisterous and energetic crowd, I forced myself to put one foot in front of the other. In my mind, a mini highlight reel of our relationship rolled behind my eyes.

I recalled when he'd invited me in his too-cocky manner to the end-of-the summer barbeque and how bone-deep my annoyance and dislike had been. *Look at me now.* The irony wasn't lost on me. Every touch, every new experience had formed an invisible thread that grew in strength and tethered us together. The more I let him in, and he did with me, the more I had learned aspects about his character that I'd never considered. His loyalty to his brother and cousins was no secret, but to be folded into that inner circle was extraordinary. I'd never needed a squad, exactly. I'd had Gia—until I didn't.

That part of our journey brought so much pain, and I wished she would open her eyes and see me for who I was. She should've. But I suspected she was going through her own, if misguided, growth journey. Maybe someday, if I could reach out to her in the distant future, she would forgive me, just as I did her.

A surge of players thundering along the sidelines made me pause and step farther from the field. I watched another play unfold from a safe distance. Our offense had lined up at the thirty-yard line. Instead of running toward the end zone, Damon provided extra coverage for the blitz, and Phoenix slipped through the line, running the ball for a touchdown that, again, brought the crowd to their feet. I swore the ground shook from the force of their reaction.

A small smile tugged at my mouth, and I squinted past the end zone as our team wasted no time lining up for the field goal. The scouts were smiling from ear to ear. And while it filled me with happiness to know they'd watched what was already a spectacular game, sadness nearly brought me to my knees. That was it for me. I couldn't deny what those last few hours meant.

I pushed out a heavy breath and straightened my shoulders with resolve. *Screw it.* I shot off a text to Riley, asking her to send me the game highlights but saying that I was out of there. I would do the interview and write the article, but staying until the end wasn't in the cards for me. Not with how much harder it felt as the scoreboard clock ticked off the remaining minutes in the game, just as I imagined it would do until Mom and I left.

CHAPTER TWENTY-THREE

SKYLAR

#Lost

The rich aroma of coffee beans pulled me from a fitful sleep. When I managed to drag myself from bed Saturday morning, I navigated the cluttered maze of boxes everywhere to get to my caffeine. That was it. Mom was serious, and we would be disappearing to parts unknown. Goodbye, scholarship and college plans at Thane University.

My soul held a bitter aftertaste as I downed coffee and helped Mom pack. We worked together all morning until guilt grew to an unbearable weight. I had to try to talk to Gia. That was why I found myself on her doorstep, ringing the bell, and I worried about the reception I would get from her parents.

Gabriella, Gia's mom, answered the door and smiled. "Sky, it's so good to see you. Come in." She stepped back and held the door open wide. The incredible smell of sauce beckoned me to enter. "Everyone misses you around here."

My shoulders relaxed, and my smile turned genuine as I stepped into the Morettis' living room, realizing that Gia hadn't told her parents what had happened. "I miss you all too." I hugged her, not wanting to go into why I hadn't been around. "Is Gia here?"

"Yes, she's in her room. Go on back."

I turned down the hall and headed to Gia's room, where music leaked from under the closed door. I knocked then entered when she yelled for me to come in. The place was a disaster, and I stepped carefully.

Clothes had been thrown on her bed, and several pairs of shoes littered the floor. The closet door stood open, revealing her list of senior goals that had started everything. I scowled at the reminder.

When she turned with another armful of shirts and saw me, they fell into a heap on the floor. "What are you doing here?"

Anger colored her words, and I braced against the betrayal and hatred flashing in her brown eyes.

"We need to talk."

She huffed then shrugged a shoulder. "I don't have anything to say to you. Leave. As you can see, I'm getting ready to go out with Tina, Rebecca, and a bunch of others from school, and you're not invited."

"They aren't your friends. They don't care about you and will drop you whenever they want or at the first sign of your popularity hanging by a thread."

She sucked in a breath like I'd physically slapped her.

"I'm popular now. *Me.* Get it through your head. I know you don't care what people think of you. It's always been like that. But they like me, and that matters. I don't need you anymore, so go away."

God, she could be mean. "Look, I gave you a pass for how you've been treating me because of what you did for Mom and me when we were little. And I know what you saw hurt you. But there's more to it, and you've never let me explain."

"You can't explain away what I saw with my own eyes. You're a shallow, backstabbing bitch, and I want you to get out of my house."

"You're calling me those things? Complete bullshit. And let's not forget who your new friends really are—the same girls who have been making fun of you since junior high. You're smarter than to hang around with them."

She snorted. "None of them slept with my boyfriend behind my back."

The more we talked, the less she seemed to listen and the angrier I got.

"I did you a favor." I stabbed my index finger in her direction. "Damon was never your boyfriend. He went along with all those fake dates because I asked him to."

The angry pink bled from Gia's cheeks, and she stumbled back to the edge of her closet door.

Regret hit me hard. *Was what I did any better than just sleeping with him?* I wasn't so sure.

"You're delusional. Damon was into me before you came around." She grabbed a chunk of her blond hair. "The day I did this, he finally saw *me*. Not *you*."

"Look"—I gentled my voice—"Damon asked me to the summer barbeque, and I told him no. After the spilled drink and the bad home dye job, I didn't want you to end up with a senior year that you regretted. I tried to help, since it was so important to you."

"I don't believe you. And whatever happened, a disloyal bitch is still a bitch." She flung her hand toward the door. "Get out. I never want to see you again."

I ran my hands through my hair. *What will it take to get through to her?* I pushed out a breath. I had nothing else I could do. "I'm going, but I also came to say goodbye. My dad will be out and probably home soon. Mom and I have to leave town because he's coming for us." I turned to go. With my back to her so I wouldn't see pity, if she had any, I stilled with my hand on the doorknob, tensed to turn it. "You're the best friend I've ever had, and I wish we could go back and do this year over." I opened the door and left with one final apology. "I never meant for you to get hurt."

CHAPTER TWENTY-FOUR

DAMON

#Brutal

The only consolation for having to say goodbye to Sky was that she and her mom would be safe. Thank God it was Saturday, and we had a fight scheduled. The unsettled feeling inside me mixed with rage, and I needed an outlet. I needed to put everything that had happened between Sky and me to bed so I could get back to my real life.

I pulled into the lot of an abandoned warehouse in the crappy part of town where we were holding the fights that time. Cole, Phoenix, and Shane were already inside, and I joined them near the Ring to watch the matches ahead of mine.

The noise inside bounced off the metal ceiling and walls, increasing in volume. Dim lights lit up the space around the Ring, and portable ones had been brought in to illuminate every inch of the mats where the fights took place. Everything about the night felt like old times, and I breathed it in, attempting to get my head on straight. Or back to what it used to be.

The smell of blood and sweat permeated the mixture of perfume and cologne from the audience. Phoenix, Shane, and I would fight, and fuck yeah, that was how it should be. I didn't need Skylar or any of the other complications from her friend. None of that was necessary.

We had a few matches to go, and the three of us would close the event that night. It made sense, since we drew the biggest crowd.

Riley had stayed at the house to hang with her mom, so I got my brother all to myself for a change. It was a risk for him to go to the fights. He'd declined last time, but whatever reason had convinced him to go to the current fight I wouldn't question.

"How's football going?" I already knew Cole was killin' it, but any additional insight about the team, or the coach, would help.

Cole's gaze shifted to me as he looked away from Darren, a wrestler who was up against some kid I didn't know. "Not gonna lie. It's tough, but I love every minute of it. Coach rides us to be the best we can be, but he's also fair. The team is great, and you guys will love living at the house."

I couldn't wait to get out of town and onto the next chapter. Of the four of us, Cole and Phoenix were the best and were driven by their goal of going into the NFL. I wanted to, and I thought Shane did as well, but I was open to other possibilities if they presented themselves.

"It can't come soon enough." I meant it. I missed Cole. "Are you and Riley getting your own place next year?"

Cole grinned, crossing his arms over his chest. "We talked about it but decided to wait until our third year. I'll buy a house, or Dad will, so we can all live there."

"You're all right if Dad buys the place we'll live in?" Because I wasn't.

Cole shrugged. "It's an investment, and after we leave, he can rent it to other college students. So no. It doesn't, and it shouldn't bother you either." His gaze sharpened. "What's going on with you? You're more on edge than usual."

"He's been spending a lot of time with that Skylar chick," Phoenix interjected, and I contemplated punching him.

"The same one who wrote the article on Riley last year?" Cole grinned, and I didn't like the knowing look in his eyes.

"Yeah," I answered. "But it's over. She's moving."

"When did this happen?" Phoenix's silver eyes widened.

"I found out about it two weeks ago." I shrugged. "It's no big deal." It was, but I barely wanted to admit that to myself. And tonight was about getting back to basics, which Skylar had no business being a part of.

So why can't I stop thinking about her?

The crowd surged forward, and a group of girls from our class surrounded us. Jessica edged near me, her arm brushing against mine. She was my go-to girl for the most part. Or she had been before Sky.

The current fight ended, and Shane entered the Ring. I ignored the girls. It wasn't any different than how it had been. Even when I caught sight of Tina and Rebecca closing in and Gia immediately behind them. Fuck that. If she came within hearing distance, I would tell her to fuck off and to get far away from me. I'd never wanted her.

The girls and the crowd faded as I cheered on Shane then Phoenix until it was finally my time in the Ring. I couldn't be more ready. The usual anger and destruction that lived inside me needed an outlet.

The guy I faced off with had a similar build and menacing shadows in his dark eyes. With the signal, the fight began, and we circled each other. I threw the first punch, and we traded off, some hitting the intended target while others were blocked. But he had rage inside him, too, and it freed more of mine.

Every time an image of Sky flashed in my mind, I hit harder and moved faster. The fight turned brutal, or more specifically, I did. It was over too soon. I didn't relish the win. I wanted more time to take out my aggression on a like-minded fighter. And even though I defeated him, I could tell my opponent felt the same.

I came out of the Ring to learn that Cole, Phoenix, and Shane planned to head to my house. Jessica clung to my side. My brother and cousins moved toward the exit, creating room that she quickly took advantage of and shifted in front of me.

She pushed her hair away from her face and tilted her head back, smiling at me. "Why don't we go somewhere and celebrate?"

"Not going to happen, Jess." I wanted her off me, and I scanned the crowd with hopes of catching sight of that bitch Gia. I wanted to lay into her. I had plenty of aggression I needed an outlet for.

Jess clung tighter to my arm, walking backward. "I heard you make deals now. What deal would you make to turn me into prom queen?"

Fuck my life. I did not have time for that shit. I shook her off, not caring if Gia's senior year list got spread all over the school. It would only reflect badly on her.

"Don't you want anything?" Jess kept pace at my side, pushing through the crowd by sticking close, digging her nails into my arm with desperation. It made me sick.

I knew what she was talking about, and before Sky, I would have been all over her. But not anymore. All I could think about was Sky. I increased my pace and ditched Jess, who got hung up in the crowd.

When I got to my truck, I found myself driving toward Sky's house. I couldn't get her out of my mind. Once on her street, I scanned the area for the car that had been stalking her, but I found nothing.

I parked at the curb then tapped on her window until she opened it and let me in. I climbed through and pulled her into my arms. Emotions warred inside me that I was helpless to do anything about.

It only made me angrier as I inhaled her intoxicating scent and growled, "I can't stop thinking about you. I need you, Skylar."

Her arms came around my neck, and she squeezed me just as tight, gasping as I took her mouth in a seductively slow kiss. After she melted against me, I pulled back, meeting her blue gaze.

"Please."

"I want you too," she said, her voice just above a whisper.

It answered everything that raged inside me, demanding more.

CHAPTER TWENTY-FIVE

SKYLAR

#NotFair

Wrapped in Damon's strong arms, our legs tangled together, I never wanted to leave. I couldn't believe we'd spent almost the entire night together. He smoothed my hair from my face and pulled me tight against him. My mind was blown by how he'd made me feel. Sex between us had always been intense and hot, but it had become something more, almost tender, like he had feelings for *me*, not just my body.

"I don't want you to leave." I could feel a deep hole primed to open in my chest when he did. "I'm afraid I'll never see you again."

"You'll forget about me." He kissed my forehead and held me a tiny bit tighter.

"Not likely. And there won't be a line of guys waiting to take your place like there are with girls willing to take mine."

He chuckled, and it rumbled through his chest and into mine. "None of them are you. And… I want you to miss me."

I tilted my head back and met his deep-blue eyes. His dark

hair was messed up in the sexiest way from when I'd run my fingers through it, and I committed the image to memory. Not that I needed to. Damon had made a lasting impression that I doubted anyone could replace.

"Mom's going to be up soon. You have to go." It pained me to say it because it physically hurt.

He kissed me so deeply that I forgot to breathe. *But do I really need oxygen when I have Damon?*

We got dressed and kissed several more times. The last ended in a hug where he squeezed me so hard, I thought he might pop my lungs. This sucked. I hated it so much.

After he climbed through the window and moved it down into place with his hands on the glass outside, I fell back onto my bed and let the tears flow.

An hour later, I stirred from a fitful nap when I heard Mom moving about in the kitchen. I looked around my room. It was almost packed.

Glass shattered, and fear drove like a knife into my gut. I yanked open my door and tiptoed to the kitchen, terrified I would find Mom in a puddle of blood. I tried to look everywhere at once for any threats but saw none. Mom stood unmoving in the kitchen, her gaze trained on the broken glass on the floor.

"Mom?" I approached with caution. "Are you okay?"

"Ahh, yeah."

But she didn't move. Her phone wasn't in her hand, so whatever had ahold of her didn't seem like it was from someone calling. *Maybe a memory?* Or she was just as overwhelmed and exhausted as me.

I didn't know what else to do, so I grabbed a broom and dustpan and got to work sweeping it up. Maybe giving her something else to focus on rather than whatever she was thinking about would help. "Have you decided on Chicago or Boston yet?"

She seemed to snap out of it and bent to help by taking the dustpan from me so I could sweep the broken shards into it.

"No. Maybe we could try the Carolinas. We would still be close enough to drive to the mountains. They get snow in higher elevations. And if we're in South Carolina, it might be easier to find an affordable place to live rather than Chicago or Boston." She stood, dumped the glass into the garbage can, then looked at me expectantly.

My pulse hammered against my skin. I didn't want to leave. Even though Gia and I were having massive issues, she was my best friend. Then there was Damon and what could be if we gave our relationship a chance to be something real—without the fake label hanging between us—if the ticking clock of my moving day weren't in the equation.

"I don't want to go." Tears fell unchecked down my face, and I shook from the overwhelming emotions crashing over me. "It's not fair. I don't want to give up everything because my dad is a psycho."

"Oh, Sky." Mom pulled me into her arms. "I hate that you're being punished because we have to hide from him." Her body shook as she cried with me. "I'm so sorry."

We dissolved into tears, indulging in the out-of-control emotions for as long as it took to release them. Then I pulled away. I grabbed a box of Kleenex, took out a few, and handed them to her. We cleaned up before moving into the family room and sitting on the couch.

"This will give us a new start." Mom's voice was clogged with emotion. "We're doing it together, and we'll be safe." She sniffed then dabbed at her nose. "I know it seems incredibly unfair, but a new life is better than a snuffed-out one. And I'm so afraid that's what'll happen if we don't leave before he gets out."

I hugged my knees to my chest. "How long until he hunts us down wherever we move, and we have to do it all over again?

We'll always have to look over our shoulders, watching and waiting for him to come for us."

Mom hiccupped, a few more tears trailing down a path already forged by the others.

"We should stay and fight. Stand our ground." I felt more confident that I could make a difference against my dad after my lessons from Damon.

She grimaced. "Is this about that boy?"

He was a big reason behind it, but I wouldn't admit that. "It's about standing up for ourselves."

"That's fine when someone doesn't want to punish you for the wrong they think you did them. But he *will* come for us." Her voice shook, and her eyes were wild with fear. "He will try to kill us. Packing and moving is our only choice. We need to finish so we can load the truck and get on the road tomorrow."

"He's not out until Tuesday, right?"

It was Sunday, and she wanted to leave by Monday, which was just so soon.

"Yes, but we need to get on the road and put as much distance between him and us as possible."

I nodded, resigned that tomorrow I would leave behind everything and everyone I'd ever known or cared about.

CHAPTER TWENTY-SIX

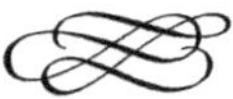

DAMON

\#NotonMyWatch

Dinner out was a mandatory affair, and no number of excuses had gotten me out of it. I sat across from my dad, surrounded by my brother, Riley, and Raelyn. It was fake as shit, but I kept my mouth shut about whatever we were pretending to be.

The interior of the American-style pub was dim, one of those places where peanut shells used to be thrown on the floor. It couldn't be done anymore—too many airborne allergies. Sports memorabilia hung on the walls, and conversation buzzed around us in the packed restaurant. We'd gone out fairly early, but the place was always busy and known for its burgers.

We'd put in our orders, and our drinks were on the table. I sipped mine. Spinach dip and potato skins would be out soon. I was more than ready for them. My stomach was trying to eat itself.

It was the last place I wanted to be—forced into conversation with my dad and Raelyn—so I kept my mouth shut and listened while they talked. Maybe I would get lucky and not have to say anything before I could leave.

"How's diving going, Riley?" Raelyn sipped her wine, her gaze locked on her daughter.

"Good. Exhausting." Riley grinned, and Cole draped an arm around the back of her chair. "An Olympic coach reached out to me the other day."

"What?" Raelyn's excitement bounced around the table in a whirl of energy. "Who is he or she? Was this at one of your meets?" She turned to my dad with a frown. "I bet it was one we couldn't go to."

"It was, but that doesn't matter." Riley shrugged then rummaged through her purse. "He gave me his card, and I asked for an extra." She handed it to my dad.

"Thanks. I'll look into him."

"Riley and I did some research, but it would help if you could vet him too," Cole said.

"How are classes and football?" Dad asked.

The appetizers arrived, and we helped ourselves to some before Cole answered. It was working out great. If they monopolized the conversation, I would happily be invisible. Anger continued to churn in me at my dad's proximity most of all. I wasn't happy around Raelyn either. I shoved a chip loaded with dip into my mouth.

"Classes are fine," Cole said. "Gen eds aren't too hard, which is good because I spend so much time in practice, the weight room, or watching tape. But I love it. I have a lot of respect for Coach Jones. He gets to know all his players, not just the starters."

"And the football house? How's that going?" Raelyn leaned back in her chair. "I was surprised you two could come back this weekend."

"It's crazy that we both have off for an extended weekend, and we wanted to watch the game. Coach Jones came to watch.

And one of his scouts." Cole slapped me on the shoulder. "You showed him something good."

"It was a great game, Damon." Dad's eyes sharpened when they landed on me.

The gig was up. I'd been dragged into the conversation. I dropped my half-eaten potato skin on the plate. "Yeah, it was. Thanks." I turned to Riley. "I know Sky was happy to sit with you. She's had to go to the home games because of writing articles for the academy's blog."

"It was fun to catch up with her." Riley's face brightened. "That girl is the only person who made my first meet even slightly easy."

"What are you talking about?" I knew Sky had written the article about her, but Riley had kicked ass. Or that was what I'd heard anyway. Cole and I hadn't dug into the shit that had gone down before it.

"She's just this badass chick who came up to me. And aside from Cass, Sky was the only other girl I felt had my back in school."

"Are you dating her?" Raelyn asked, and I glared.

"Damon."

Dad's warning only churned the ember of anger inside me to a roaring blaze.

"When have you ever known me to date anyone?" I shifted my gaze to my dad, and everything in me hardened. "It seems I'm more like you in that area."

His jaw clenched, and Raelyn and Riley exchanged glances. Cole finished the dip, ignoring my outburst and Dad's pissed-off expression.

The waitress chose that moment to deliver our entrées. No one said anything while dishes were put in front of us. It wasn't until we were alone again that Dad opened his mouth to snap back, but Raelyn put her hand on his forearm and squeezed. He pushed out a breath then let it go.

We needed to get through the next half hour without a raging fight. I picked up my burger and took a large bite to keep my mouth busy before I said more. Like how cute it was that we were out together, playing at a happy family when we'd buried our mom a little over a year ago.

Isn't it funny how quickly past mistakes are ignored, like in this moment? I chewed on the thought.

A visual sweep around the pub distracted me while I inhaled my food. Cole and Riley picked up the conversation. I lost interest in even attempting to be a part of it by listening.

Somehow, I got through dinner, excusing myself to use the restroom while Dad took care of the check. After washing my hands, I exited, not expecting to find him leaning against the wall in the hallway, his hands casually stuffed into his pockets.

"We're doin' this?" I didn't care how I sounded. I couldn't quiet my anger around him.

"I've talked to you about your attitude toward Raelyn before. But no, I'm not going to address that here. Instead, I want you to tell me what's happening with school, football, or even that girl. Because something other than our family dynamic is eating at you, and you need to address it."

A slow smile spread across my mouth, and Dad's eyes turned stormy. It wasn't a friendly smile, and he was right to anticipate some bullshit from me.

I wanted to flip the tables and get him thinking, and I spoke without considering what came out of my mouth. "Why did you push Cole so hard to take business classes? To get involved with your company? Not once did you say anything to me."

His eyes widened a fraction. Not enough that anyone else would notice, but I did, and it told me how much I'd shocked him.

"I pushed Cole because I worried he wouldn't have a backup plan for football. Life happens." He shrugged the one shoulder not resting against the wall. "I didn't want to see him struggle if he got a career-ending injury or—"

"Got a girl pregnant." I was tense. I needed to hit something or someone.

He gave a slow nod. "Or that."

"And me? Don't you have any concerns that I'll fuck things up?"

"That wasn't why. You and Cole are both so similar and also different. You breeze through classes and get high marks without much studying. And your classes were already geared toward law. I knew you wanted to be involved in the business by what you took and how you argued a point. I didn't realize you saw my lack of pushing as uninterest or that I didn't care about what you did with your life."

"Don't look too deep into it." Some of the anger dissipated, but I was still restless. "I'm going back to the table. We're done here, right?"

He nodded slowly. I ignored the speculative gleam in his eyes as I brushed past him and returned to the table long enough to say my goodbyes.

I loved my brother and Riley, but spending Sunday with my dad and Raelyn had every one of my nerves strung tight. I bailed on dessert and went to our cousins while Cole and Riley decided to go to a movie or on some date-night thing.

Phoenix texted that they were in the basement, and after letting myself in, I went downstairs. My lousy mood went to shit when I saw Shane's girlfriend, Tracey. The blond Barbie wannabe had Shane whipped, and the rest of us were just waiting for him to come to his senses.

Water in hand, Tracey leaned against the back of the couch while Phoenix and Shane played a video game.

"Ran into Jessica," Tracey said. "She thinks you're still hung up on that nerd-girl, Skylar." Her gaze skimmed me up and down. "She's a nobody and dresses like one too. I have plenty of friends I can set you up with so you don't have to scrape the scum from the bottom of the barrel."

"Shut the fuck up about Sky. And the last thing I want is someone like you who fucks her way to the pro-wives' club."

"You don't know anything." She flicked her hair over her shoulder.

"Aaron Jamison? Ring a bell?"

She scowled. I'd hit a nerve, and I noticed Phoenix watching Shane, not the TV. He hated Tracey the most out of all of us.

"If Aaron hadn't torn his rotator cuff, he'd still be a viable option," I stated. "But that injury kicked him off the fuckable-for-money list, and you dumped him."

"Right. You know everything about a relationship you were never in." She rolled her eyes and jammed her hand on her hip.

"Why don't you just admit it?" I goaded.

"Admit what? I have nothing to hide." Her chin tilted higher, and hatred flashed in her eyes. She didn't have to mask it because Shane wasn't paying attention.

"It's no secret that you only date guys you think will be college draft picks. And with Shane's stats, he's almost guaranteed a first-round spot."

"You know nothing about Shane and me. Keep your ridiculous opinions to yourself."

"Funny. You didn't do that with Sky. But then again, if I'm with one of your friends, she'll have a spot with you in the pro-wives' club."

"You're such an asshole."

I laughed, feeling better. Getting under Tracey's skin was worth the aggravation of having her there in the first place.

"Break it up." Shane tossed his remote on the table in front of the couch, and Tracey went to sit next to him like the dutiful girlfriend she pretended to be. He swiveled on the couch to face me. "What the fuck is going on with you?"

Phoenix shot me a grimace. He didn't agree, but knowing

him, he was biding his time with his brother and figuring out how to get Tracey out of the picture. I didn't have the patience for that shit. Nor did I care.

"Fuck off." I was out of there.

I wanted to slam out of the house, but my aunt had most likely worked the graveyard shift at the hospital and was sleeping. After quietly leaving, I got into my SUV and drove around, needing time to think.

There had to be a way to help Sky and her mom. I didn't want her to leave. Maybe if I talked to them both, I could change their minds.

An hour later, I found myself on Sky's street. I parked down the block then texted her to come out, wanting to see her again before she left. Hand on my car door handle, I froze as the old black Camaro that I'd spotted once before in front of her house stopped and parked.

The door opened, and a tall, lanky guy dressed in dark jeans and a black front-zippered hoodie stepped out looking sketchy as hell. Sky was going to open the door to a threat if I didn't do something.

I got out, my hands balled into fists, and followed him, ready for a fight.

CHAPTER TWENTY-SEVEN

SKYLAR

#EarlyRelease

A crash sounded then the thud of a fist against flesh. My heart jackhammered against my ribs as I opened the front door. The light cut through the inky darkness to show Damon had some guy pinned to the ground, raining punches on his face.

When I rushed onto the porch, Damon lifted his gaze to mine. "Call 911!"

Shit. My phone was on the kitchen counter. I sprinted inside as Mom passed by to see what was going on. I typed in my passcode and raced outside.

"Stop!" Mom yelled.

I burst through the door to find Mom clinging to Damon's bicep. She couldn't have stopped him, but he had enough sense to pause.

I swiped my phone's screen to eliminate the partially dialed emergency call. "What's going on?"

The guy on the ground had his hands raised by his face, but when Damon stood, the guy scurried to his feet, putting space between them. I barely stopped myself from snorting at that move. I couldn't blame him. I'd seen the damage Damon could do at those stupid underground fights.

Mom stepped in front of the guy, her gaze darting from Damon to me and back again. "This is Jace Bellinger. He's a private security guy I hired to keep an eye on Skylar and the house."

I crossed my arms over my chest and growled. "You could have told me. He's the guy from the car I told you about. All that ended up doing was scaring me, Mom." I addressed her but glared at him. *Asshole.* He probably knew he'd scared the hell out of me.

"Didn't do a very good job, then. I saw you sneaking up to the house." Damon shifted to position himself slightly in front of me.

Mom smiled, softening more toward Damon. Too bad we were leaving, because his actions of late had brought her over to his side. And that would have come in handy for me when I wanted to spend time with him.

"That was very brave of you, Damon. But Jace is one of the good guys. He's been keeping an eye on things in case Adam happened to show up."

"Which is the reason I'm here," Jace said, taking a step back to add more distance between him and Damon.

I couldn't blame him. His black eye and split lip, as opposed to the lack of anything on Damon's, told an accurate story of who had been winning the fight, and it wasn't the grown professional security man.

Mom turned to face Jace, ignoring Damon and me. When Mom stiffened, I moved closer and grabbed her hand for support.

"Adam was released early. Friday, to be exact. Somehow his release status got delayed in the system, so I just learned of it. He bought a bus ticket to Seattle this morning."

"His family is in Seattle," Mom said.

"Wait. What family?" It stung to know Mom had been aware that I had living grandparents and had never trusted me with the information. Then another thought followed, and hope rose inside me. "Does that mean we can stay?"

Mom squeezed my hand, worry lining the corners of her mouth. "No. I'm sorry, honey. His family is wealthy, and he's probably going to them to get access to his accounts. They had some fancy lawyer who cut me off from accessing them. His parents are in control of his accounts and the money he made in the MLB."

"But why do we have to leave if he's there?" I argued.

Mom cupped my shoulder briefly. "He's probably getting money to live on while he returns to terrorize us. And his parents will act as his alibi. They've done it before."

When Mom turned back to Jace, I grabbed Damon's hand and pulled him into the house. I was confused and irritated but didn't want to take it out on Mom. She was already a mess about my dad.

I was more hurt than anything after hearing that I had grandparents. Ones that didn't care about us at all. I had been only seven when Dad had gone to prison, and as far as I knew, they'd never tried to help us in any way.

"Your dad was a professional athlete?" Damon broke into my destructive train of thought.

"Yeah, and a total piece of shit," I shot back.

"So much makes sense now," he mumbled.

"Whatever." I was annoyed.

"That's why you hate athletes." His face held no judgment.

I pushed aside my irritation. "Yes."

"And now?" He crowded me against the counter, his dark-blue eyes heating with desire.

I shrugged. "I might like one or two."

His eyebrows rose. "Two?"

"Riley." I laughed as the agitation faded from his expression. The guy was alpha, but I'd grown to like that about him. My smile fell, and I placed my hand against his cheek as a thrill of excitement and overwhelming emotion swarmed me. "Thank you."

"For what?" His gaze dropped to my lips.

"Fighting to keep my mom and me safe." I brushed my lips across his in a soft caress then pulled back, my hand on his chest to let him know I wasn't ready for him to take control. Not yet. "Why were you here?"

"I wanted to see you." He tucked some hair behind my ear, his fingers grazing my cheek. "I hate that you're leaving."

Tears misted my eyes, blurring my vision. I hated crying, and I blinked them back furiously. "I do too."

"My dad is a lawyer. He could help."

If only. I shook my head. "Thanks, but Mom's been down the legal road before. And I've watched enough TV to know that guys like my dad don't care about the law or pieces of paper that state they can't come near us."

"I don't think hiding is much better. If his parents are wealthy, or he is, he could find you."

"I agree with you, but I don't have a choice."

"You do." His eyes burned with determination. "You could stay and fight. Guys like your dad don't like it when someone fights back."

A sad smile curved my lips. It was a no-win situation for us. "I'm afraid he'll kill Mom or me if we fight back. I've been over this with her enough already, and she's terrified. Damon, she almost didn't make it last time he attacked her. I can't take that risk just because I don't want to leave you."

I could see the argument poised on the tip of his tongue by how his eyes flashed. So I did the only thing I knew would work if I wanted to shut him up. I wrapped my arms around his neck and kissed him.

When we broke apart, I felt like I was losing part of myself by leaving him.

"I'll miss you." My voice shook, and I inhaled slowly, trying to maintain control of the emotions raging inside me. I flattened my palms on his chest, loving the feel of his heart racing beneath one hand. "Maybe someday we'll find each other again." It was the only thought that would keep me going. That if things were meant to be, then they would be.

I walked him to the front door and kissed him goodbye. It wasn't until he left that I dissolved into a messy puddle of tears, hating how drastic things had to be to avoid Mom and me dying.

CHAPTER TWENTY-EIGHT

DAMON

#AskingforHelp

When I parked in the garage, it was well past midnight. I slammed the car door and went inside, where I stood in the kitchen, feeling helpless and frustrated. Every time I shut my eyes, Sky's gorgeous face appeared. I could almost hear her laugh, which lit up every part of my worthless soul. But then the fear that had darkened her eyes appeared, and I wanted to banish it.

I would miss her so goddammed much. And I had to find a way to help her. I couldn't ignore the all-consuming need to keep her safe, which I couldn't do if she left. On that note, I didn't even know where they planned to go.

I shoved my fingers through my hair, anger crackling like a live wire. I didn't have a choice. I had to ask my dad for help. He was a corporate lawyer, not a family or criminal one, but he had guys at his firm who could help. It was the only thing I could think of, and I wanted to tell Sky and her mom that they had options besides running away.

With no other ideas, I hurried up the stairs to Dad's room, softly knocked on the door, and waited. No way would I barge in there to find out if he and Raelyn were doing something I didn't want to see. When no sound came from behind the door, I knocked a little louder.

Rustling followed, then the door opened, and Dad appeared, blinking against the light in the hallway. "What's going on?" He stepped into the hallway and shut the door behind him, probably so we wouldn't wake Raelyn.

The door opened, and she joined us anyway, a silk robe sinched tightly around her waist. I ignored her. Dad took her hand in his. Fine, if she wanted to listen, whatever.

"I have a friend"—she was so much more than that—"who needs help."

"This is a legal matter?" Dad sounded reserved, but he headed toward his study, which told me he would at least listen.

I followed and sat across from his desk. Raelyn occupied another chair in my peripheral vision.

I filled him in on everything I knew about Sky's dad and how she and her mom planned to run away because they thought the guy would kill them if they stayed. "From what I gather, Sky's mom spent years being abused, and this is her way to take back power. And stay alive."

Dad steepled his hands and blew out a breath. "The decision to leave isn't Sky's mother running away. It's her trying to protect her daughter."

I clipped a nod, not knowing what else I could do to convince him to help.

"Do you care for this girl?"

Fuck, I do. I've never felt this way before. I couldn't even deny or deflect it with a dig about caring more than he did for Mom. "Yes." I nodded. "I do."

Dad studied me. Whatever he must have seen in my expression convinced him because he nodded too. "What's the guy's name?"

"Adam McCormick. He used to play in the MLB."

He typed Sky's dad's name into his computer, and I went around the desk so I could read it too. When the charges popped up, I felt sick.

"There are pictures." Dad clicked on a tab, and photos filled the screen.

Holy fuck. They were pictures of Sky when she was young along with her mother. They were bad. Her mom was unrecognizable, and there was so much blood. The side of Sky's face was discolored, and a gash bled by her temple. She'd said her dad had beat her mom, but she hadn't explained how badly he'd beaten her too.

I had to look away and breathed slowly through my nose. My hands fisted at my sides. I wanted to kill the bastard who did that to Sky.

"Have them move in here, with us," Raelyn said.

My head swung toward her, and she flicked her eyes to my dad's before looking back at me.

"We can get security and keep them safe while your dad finds a loophole to get Sky's father to stay away," she added.

It didn't escape my notice that she would feel a connection to the situation Sky and her mom faced. She and Riley had endured a similar experience. A grudging sense of respect pushed aside some of my hate toward her.

"You would do that?" I asked. "Let two strangers come stay with us because I asked?"

She tilted her chin up, and determination flashed in her eyes. "Of course I would."

"Dad?" While I appreciated her show of support more than I cared to examine at the moment, my dad had the ultimate say about whether our intervention would do any good. "Would that work? Can we do something?"

"I'm sorry, Damon. We can't do much to help them. Not at this point. The best thing you can do for her is let her go."

I didn't want to accept that, even if it was true.

CHAPTER TWENTY-NINE

SKYLAR

#MovingSucks

I *love Damon. Honestly, what were the odds that I would fall for him?* I swiped angrily at my eyes, wiping away more stupid tears. We didn't even like each other. It was that damn attraction. I couldn't deny it when he touched me.

Gia's stupid senior-year list had brought us together in the first place. If it weren't for that, I would have continued to turn down any invitation or demand he laid out for me. I'd promised him a favor to make her dreams come true.

And he had.

The crazy thing was, he'd made dreams come true for me, too, ones I wasn't even aware I had. We had finally reached a place where we talked to each other, and it was coming to an end because of my dad.

I saw no point in sleeping. I didn't even try. Once we got to wherever Mom decided, I would sleep for a week. The time on my phone read one in the morning, and as I glanced around my room, I was amazed to find that everything I owned fit into five boxes.

The rest of the rooms weren't much more. After twenty years of living there, since my parents had moved before I was born, our entire house would fit into one medium-sized truck. There should be more. I thought I remembered more, but Mom must've purged over the years in case we had to leave in a hurry.

I sat on my bed, mentally exhausted. It felt weird in the house. The TV was on in the family room, and I heard Mom moving around in her bedroom, packing. The security guy was parked outside, which gave Mom confidence, especially after he'd offered to install a camera at the back door while he watched the front. Mom had jumped at the chance. In addition, our backyard was lit up like a summer day from the overly bright lightbulbs.

I didn't see why, since my dad was on a bus to Seattle. But they'd explained that it served a point. If Dad came to the house, even after we moved, he would be caught violating the restraining order, and we could send him back to prison.

My heart hurt so bad. I hated that we were leaving and that I might never see Damon again. When my phone pinged, I couldn't help but smile. It was from Damon, asking if I was okay. He must've sensed me thinking about him.

I replied that I was.

Instead of texting me back, he called. "I looked up your dad, and as much as I hate to say it, your mom is probably right to want to leave town."

"Yeah, but it still sucks."

"It does. Do you want me to come over?"

His deep voice made me shiver.

"I could come over and stand guard," he offered.

I wanted that more than anything, but I couldn't let him. "Thanks, but no. I can't handle saying goodbye again."

"I'll be here if you need me. It doesn't matter where you go. Call me, and I'll come for you."

"I'll miss you."

We said goodbye, and I burst into tears as soon as we hung up. It felt like the worst thing imaginable. I swiped a box of Kleenex I hadn't yet packed from my nightstand and tried to clean my face.

Glass shattered in the other room. Mom must've dropped another drinking glass.

I left my room, sniffling and using the tips of my fingers to swipe beneath my eyes to clear away the last few stubborn tears. The day sucked. I stopped in the bathroom to splash some water on my face, in no hurry to rush to the mess from whatever Mom had dropped in the kitchen.

The cold water eased a tiny bit of the ache from my unwanted emotions. I stuck my wrists under the cool stream. With a twist, I shut it off then wiped my face with a towel and dried my eyes. I couldn't stall anymore and went to help Mom clean up. At the end of the hallway, my gaze went to the kitchen, where I thought Mom would be with a broom.

It was empty except for a slew of packed boxes. An eerie silence hung in the space, thick with tension. "Mom?" My skin prickled with a sickening suspicion that something was wrong, and I turned toward the family room.

Then I saw him. My heart skipped a beat, and my fingers tingled from the shock. Time moved sluggishly, the pieces of the picture before me registering oddly in my brain.

A large man stood in the middle of the living room. Pressure built in my chest. In less than a second, I cataloged everything. Mom was on the couch with tears tracking down her cheeks. Glass from the window lay scattered around the man's feet. He had impossibly broad shoulders, muscular biceps covered with tattoos, and short light-brown hair. But the cold brown eyes and hard slash of lips bracketed by angry lines triggered my memory the most.

I couldn't contain the pressure any longer, and I screamed.

Dad had found us.

CHAPTER THIRTY

DAMON

\#OverBeforeItStarted

Cole leaned against my door, waiting for me to disconnect with Sky. When I did, he came in, concern darkening his green eyes.

"Riley asleep?" I tossed my phone on my desk and ran my hands through my hair, wishing I could think of a way to help Sky.

"Yeah." He sat on the couch in my room and turned toward me. "What's going on?"

"Sky's moving because her dad is a threat." I filled him in on everything I knew, including that I'd asked Dad for help.

"Is she in immediate danger?"

We exchanged a knowing look because we'd been there before. My talking with Dad told Cole just what Sky meant to me.

"I hope not," I said. "They're leaving in the morning, and the security guy Sky's mom hired said her dad is on a bus to Seattle. But I'm not sure that's true. He could have bought the ticket and not gotten on the bus."

"It would be a good alibi, especially if he had someone with a similar build take his place and shield their face from any cameras."

"Right." I stood and paced. "Not helping, especially with how dangerous her father is." I stopped and met his concerned gaze. "Dad pulled up the pictures from when Adam was arrested. Sky's mom was unrecognizable, he beat her so brutally. And Sky, she was little, but he'd hit her too. I don't understand how she could forget that kind of experience. She only told me he gave her that small scar over her eyebrow."

"You said she was little. Maybe her mind blocked the trauma."

"That makes sense. I just—"

My phone buzzed, and I froze when I glanced at it. An instant sense of foreboding hit me. Gia was calling. Something was happening at Sky's house. *Fuck that.*

I answered. "What's happening?" I demanded.

"I don't know what to do. Can you come here? There's yelling at Sky's, and I thought I heard something break." Her voice shook. "She told me her dad is getting out. What if it's him?"

"Call 911 now."

I hung up then shoved my phone into my pocket. "He's there." I was out of my room and running to the garage with Cole on my heels. We got into my SUV and peeled out of the garage and onto the street. Cole called Dad and hit the speaker button.

"Cole? What's going on?" Dad's voice boomed through the car's interior.

"Damon got a call about a fight at Sky's house. We're headed there now. The neighbor is calling the cops, but—"

"Stay in the car when you get there." The scrape of keys against a hard surface sounded. Then a door slammed. "What's the address?"

I rattled it off then careened around a corner.

"I'm on my way." Authority threaded those few words before the line went dead.

Something in me settled, knowing he would help. But there was no way I would stay in the car.

"You would think a cop would be around." I flew down the street, and of course, that was the night of all nights for a cop not to be around to chase me.

The streets were empty. I sped by dark houses and under streetlamps. My headlights stretched to her home before I pulled up to the curb. The lights were on inside, but all the curtains and blinds were closed. I couldn't see anything.

A lone car was parked a house away from theirs across the street. I could barely make out a figure in the driver's seat. Probably the security guy. I wouldn't waste time on him. The guy was worthless in a fight. Cole and I got out, closing the doors as quietly as possible so we wouldn't alert her dad to our approach.

"I'll go around back and make noise, try to draw them out of the house when I think you're in position," Cole said.

We both headed toward the back, and Cole's eyebrows rose.

"I'm going in Sky's bedroom window," I said.

Cole nodded then sprinted around the corner. I flattened my hands on the cool glass and pushed upward, hoping like hell that she'd left it unlocked earlier. I shoved my fingers into the gap and pushed when it eased up an inch. Angry voices volleyed back and forth, faint before I opened the window but growing louder.

Movement beside me drew my attention, and I whirled, arm cocked.

"It's me," Gia hissed, her eyes wide with fright.

"Go home." I didn't have time for her. Carefully parting the curtains, I peeked into Sky's empty room. I didn't think they would be there. I quickly climbed inside.

Gia's leg poked through the window opening a moment later as she struggled to climb in.

Oh, for fuck's sake. "Get outta here, Gia."

"No." She glared. "Sky's my best friend, and I won't let anyone hurt her."

Does she hear the irony? I grabbed her and lifted her through. "Stay behind me."

The words grew clear as I quietly made my way down the hallway, muffled sobbing a background noise interspersed with "I'm sorry." It was Sky's mom. I recognized her voice.

"Bullshit. You tried to take my daughter away from me." The angry voice had to be Sky's dad. "You'll pay for everything you've done. All the years I've been locked away. The betrayal. Poisoning my daughter's mind against me."

"No, Daddy," Sky pleaded. "She didn't. I'm here. I'll go with you."

Over my dead body. I eased around the corner, not knowing what I would interrupt. I couldn't rush in if he held either of them at gunpoint. Her dad hovered over Sky and her mom, shouting and intimidating them as they huddled together on the couch.

The need to get him away from them nearly overrode the very real threat of ambushing him too early and causing Sky or her mom harm in the process.

"I never meant to hurt you before, baby," her dad crooned.

Before—meaning he was okay with hurting Sky now?

"But you did," she whispered. "And you're hurting me now by what you're doing to Mom."

No, Sky. Wrong method.

Things were spiraling out of control too fast. I inched closer, and horror filled me at the sound of a loud thud followed by a whimper.

CHAPTER THIRTY-ONE

SKYLAR

#DaddyIsHome

Everything was a mess. I didn't know what to do. Mom was crying as she huddled on the couch, cradling her bruised cheek from where Dad had hit her. For that alone, I hated him. *Was he always this way? A giant bully that preyed on Mom and me?* I couldn't remember. *Before the terrible way he beat Mom that got him arrested, were there good times?*

My thoughts strayed to Gia's dad and how he'd always protected his daughter. If he felt anyone had wronged Gia in any way, he got angry. He would call the kid's parents and ban the kid from coming over, which was one reason Gia had kept a lot of the school bullying she'd experienced a secret. She'd said it was embarrassing when her father did that.

I would have given anything to experience what she had with her dad because I'd grown up without one. Mom was fierce and would go to battle for me if I ever needed it, but I never did. That didn't mean things had been easy. They hadn't been. She worked like crazy, and I hated that she was alone.

I didn't care what people thought. I never had. Insults rolled off me. People's opinions didn't matter. All I cared about were the people I let into my heart. Gia was one of them. And that was why the way she'd treated me had been so painful. The others who had followed her lead didn't matter. I couldn't care less. It was Gia's insults that had cut me to the bone.

Dad ranted about how Mom had turned me against him, and I was confused. *Why would he think that? Were there bad times before that one incident?* Mom never talked about him or what he was like. *Why can't I remember?*

I hardly recognized the man standing too close to us, menace practically vibrating from him and filling me with concern. The situation was beyond fucked, but something wasn't right with my memories, or the lack of them. Something tickled the back of my mind, nagging me. I felt the box where I shoved all the bad shit crack open. *Am I ready for this?*

"I mailed her letters, and she never wrote back!" he yelled at Mom. "Where the fuck are they?"

I snapped back to the present and our ugly situation.

"Sky did write you," Mom answered. "The prison must have—"

He hauled Mom off the couch by her hair then backhanded her so hard her head whipped to the right, her body helplessly following. She lay crumpled on the ground.

I leaped up and stood between them, trying to defuse the situation. "I'm here. I'll go with you. Just us."

"You never brought her to visit!" He directed his menacing accusation at Mom.

He was screaming, and that Pandora's box opened a little more.

"I wasn't allowed to go. The courts wouldn't let me." I drew his attention away from Mom, making things up as I went.

His dark gaze swung to mine, and I held my breath at the madness swirling there.

"Come closer."

I felt sick. Fear harvested roots, and I didn't budge.

"Did your mama make you scared of me?" His hard eyes flashed hatred.

"No." I broke free of the binds trying to keep me a safe distance from him, and I took a small step forward.

I studied him. We looked nothing alike. His light-brown hair was cropped close to his head and longer on top. His eyes were smaller and dark. I didn't think his build had changed much, since he still had that athletic look, but maybe the ink was new. Something stained his shirt, and I squinted to make out what it was.

"Is that blood?"

"Yeah," he sneered then kicked Mom, who whimpered.

I lurched forward, putting myself further in front of Mom.

Sick amusement at my attempt to protect her painted his lips in a twisted grin. "I had to take care of Mama's new friend outside."

"Did you hurt Jace?"

Violence rolled off him in waves. "Are you concerned about your mama's new boyfriend?" His hand encircled my arm like a vise, and he jerked me close.

Everything I'd learned from Damon went out the window. The only thing I could think of was to keep him talking and try to calm him down. "I missed you." I forced myself to relax in his too-tight grip. "I'm so glad you're home. We can be a family again."

"I'm not sure that's in the cards," he growled and shook me.

"Adam," Mom moaned.

I stumbled back, free from his bruising grip. I couldn't be happy, though, because he went for Mom instead. His arm cocked back, and he swung as I jumped between them. Stars burst behind my eyes, followed by pain. I fell back, partially over Mom, and onto the couch.

Pandora's box exploded inside my mind in a wash of terror. I remembered everything with perfect clarity. The abuse, the hiding, the yelling and crying, and Mom being hurt. It all came back. The worst was when I'd thought he'd killed Mom. I'd gone to her, screaming and crying, only to have him hit me so hard I'd flown off my feet. I'd run and hid in Gia's treehouse.

When Gia's mom had found me, she'd been so upset. The police had come. They had taken my dad away, and my unconscious, bloody, and broken mom had been rushed to the hospital.

That bastard. Screw trying to appease him. I wanted him gone by any means possible. With a hard shove off the couch, I stood and scanned the area for anything that I could use as a weapon.

He noted my change in demeanor, and a sick smile curved his thin lips. "Good. Get angry. You're more like me than I thought."

Gross. Having anything in common with him made me sick to my stomach. *How could I have blocked out my memories of him?* "I'm nothing like you," I sneered just as I spotted a knife on the peninsula. *If I could just get to it before him...*

A crash sounded outside from the back. A few seconds later, red and blue lights painted the walls through the slight opening in the curtains.

It was enough to send him over the edge as he roared, "Who the fuck called the police?"

We both lunged for the knife. I never stood a chance against his longer legs or reach. He grabbed it then me and shoved me roughly down to the floor by Mom. I scrambled to get up but froze on the balls of my feet when the knife caught the light, gleaming as he pointed it at me.

CHAPTER THIRTY-TWO

DAMON

#Distraction

A crash sounded from the backyard. *Perfect timing, Cole.* Urgency surged through me at the unmistakable thud of a fist hitting flesh. I rushed from the edge of the hallway to find Sky on the ground with her mom. Adam stood over them, a knife pointed in their direction. Red and blue cut through the sliver in the curtains. The police arriving had provided the perfect distraction. When Adam turned toward the front window, I lunged forward and tackled him to the ground.

We rolled, and a burning sensation ripped across my shoulder. Struggling for control, I managed to pin him beneath me. The guy was strong. My fist slammed into his face. Sky slid over to us and grabbed his arm, pinning the knife with her weight. He roared and tossed Sky away, but she'd managed to loosen his grip on the knife. She must have bitten him.

She scurried back, her foot kicking the weapon out of his range. With both arms free, he kidney punched me. I didn't let it faze me. My fist cracked into his face, splattering blood as a cut opened above his eye.

Footsteps pounded on the wood floor as Cole burst in from the back of the house. Another punch then the front door opened, slamming against the wall as several cops poured into the room. The cops hauled me off Adam.

"Stop!" Sky screamed. "Let him go. He's the good guy."

Her blue eyes were wild as she ran to me just as the cops released me. Her slight weight slammed into my chest, and I wrapped my arms around her tightly. Sensing her father's intent, I stepped back quickly. He jumped to his feet with a roar. A tremor ripped through Sky, and I pivoted so he would hit me, not her. Just before her father made contact, one of the officers wrapped an arm around Adam's shoulder. Threading his free arm through Adam's opposite armpit, the officer held him in place. Another officer helped to secure Adam by gripping his forearm and wrenching it back. The metal clicks of the cuffs sounded as they were slapped onto his wrists.

With Adam sufficiently subdued, I ignored the death glare he leveled at me and scanned the rest of the room. Cole stood off to the side with another officer, helping Sky's mom off the floor. The men restraining Adam hauled him away in handcuffs.

The police collected the knife from the floor for evidence just as Dad and Raelyn walked in, followed closely by two other people that had to be Gia's parents.

"Damon." Tears rolled down Sky's face as she clung to me. "I'm sorry. Holy shit. I was so scared." Her body shook, sobs making her words nearly incoherent.

I squeezed her tighter and smoothed her hair down her back with my good arm. Pain radiated along my other shoulder, and I felt the trickle of blood running down my arm. "Everything's okay." The words were in part for me. "Fuck, when I saw the knife..."

I couldn't finish the thought. If he'd hurt her any worse than he already had, there was no telling what I would have done. As it was, I didn't know if I would've stopped. The only things that had kept me in check were how close Sky had been and that the police had pulled me off him.

She pulled back, emotion pouring from her wide eyes as she framed my face with trembling hands. "I love you."

Her words were whispered, but they went straight to my heart. The thought of losing her had driven home the same realization within me, and I smiled, my soul lighter for it. "I love you too."

I wanted to stay like that with her secure and safe in my arms, but the officer who'd pulled me off Adam motioned for me to come with him.

"We need to take a look at your arm." The older officer stood close, grimly observing the scene around us. Sirens pierced the night as more emergency vehicles arrived.

I brushed my lips over Sky's in a reassuring kiss before releasing her to go where the officer gestured.

An ambulance pulled up. From the gaping front door, I could make out the lone car I'd noticed when I'd arrived. They must have opened the door because the interior light illuminated Jace, the security guy Sky's mom had hired. He didn't look too great slumped over in his seat. The paramedics didn't rush to help him, which told me more than I cared to know.

As I moved away with the officer to get checked out, Gia hugged Sky. Sky's mom and I were directed to the paramedics as Adam was read his rights and secured in the back of a squad car.

Sky's mom climbed into one ambulance, and I sat on the back of another while the paramedic cut my shirt away at my shoulder to assess the knife wound. The sting of disinfectant drew my gaze to him for a brief moment.

"It's not bad," the paramedic said. "Mostly superficial, but you should get a full checkup because of what happened tonight."

For documentation. I was on board with that. Dad had been

talking to the cops while Raelyn and Gia's parents stood with Sky's mom. Dad must have finished because he headed toward me with Cole.

"That was foolish to run in there like you did, son."

I said nothing. He shouldn't be surprised, since both his kids had done something similar to protect the women we loved.

He signed then ran a hand through his dark hair, looking so much like Cole at that moment that it was eerie. "I'm glad you're okay. I talked with the officer in charge, and Adam McCormick will go straight back to prison without bail."

Good. I caught Sky's piercing gaze as she watched me from her mom's side. We would talk at the hospital before long. With her father out of the picture, she wouldn't have to move anywhere.

CHAPTER THIRTY-THREE

SKYLAR

#MakingUp

Gia's room was a disaster, and I laughed when I tripped over a sandal. "Why? There's no way you would wear this tonight." I had never understood her method of getting ready.

She shrugged and smoothed her recently straightened and touched-up—thanks to Mom—blond hair. "It's a process." She set the mascara tube on the counter and met my gaze in the mirror. "How are you doing?"

I rolled my eyes. "I'm fine. It's been weeks—I'm still not sure how it's October. My dad's locked up, and we don't have to move."

"Yeah, but"—she bit her bottom lip—"he killed that guy your mom hired to keep you safe. Doesn't that freak you out?"

I leaned against her bathroom door, and she turned to face me so we weren't talking to each other in the mirror anymore.

"Yes, of course, it does. But at least it wasn't for nothing." I grimaced because it was a horrible way of looking at Jace Bellinger's death. "My dad was charged with murder because of it, not just the attempted murder charge for Mom and me. And since Damon's dad and his criminal lawyers have been helping Mom with anything legal she needs, we're in a much better position."

A month had passed since Dad was taken back to jail, and even if he tried to plead guilty and strike a deal, the courts wouldn't lighten his sentence with Lucas Savage's team of lawyers on the case. Dad's phone privileges had also been revoked, so we didn't even need to worry about him trying to call us. We had still changed our numbers and made sure they were unlisted, but it helped to ease our minds, especially Mom's.

"I don't want to talk about my dad anymore."

Gia laughed then tugged on the hem of my dress. "I can't believe we're going to homecoming together, and you're wearing a dress." She squealed the last word.

I rolled my eyes. It was a sexy little black A-line dress. "Yeah, well, this is sort of our first real date." Butterflies took flight in my stomach. I couldn't believe it. Damon and I were officially dating, and I couldn't be happier.

It was funny because we'd spent almost every day together since he'd saved me. And it was his first football game back on the field since his injury. I'd had to do the write-up about it for the blog, and that was why I'd been late arriving at Gia's to get ready together, not that I fussed over my appearance that much. A swipe of mascara and a touch of lipstick were all I cared to wear.

"It's weird in a way." Her hand found her curvy hip, and she tilted her head to the side. "You ending up with Damon and me with Tucker."

Uh-oh. Things had been cool between us ever since the night my dad had broken in. Gia and I'd had plenty of discussions about what had gone on since the summer barbecue at Phoenix and Shane's—where everything had begun with her fixation on her four-point senior plan and Damon as the catalyst to kick it off.

Part of her terrible behavior toward me had been because she'd gotten so hurt. The rest had come from fear of being bullied again by the girls she had become pseudo-friends with. Once she'd come clean to me, I'd talked to Damon, and he'd made it clear to those girls that they would have the worst year of their high school careers if they did anything to Gia or me. His cousins had backed him up and effectively stopped anything before it began.

"Gia."

"What?" She grinned, the dreamy look on her face clearing slightly.

"Why is it weird that I ended up with Damon and you with Tucker?"

"Just how things worked out. I thought I was so into Damon, but it was really the stupid popularity I wanted. He never liked me, and I would have seen it if I'd pulled my head out of the clouds. But Tucker"—she sighed—"I've liked him for years. He's sweet and cute and makes me feel beautiful."

I laughed because Tucker was amazing, which was why we were friends. But Damon had stolen my heart along the way and was the perfect guy for me.

"Damon's a shoo-in for homecoming king."

I shrugged. I'd never cared about that stuff. "You've got a pretty good chance at homecoming queen."

Gia laughed before turning back to the mirror and picking up the mascara to finish. "I thought stuff like that mattered to me"—her eyes flicked to mine again—"but it doesn't. Homecoming queen, or prom queen, like I had on my senior list, isn't that important anymore. Spending time and making memories with my best friend and boyfriend are what's important. I don't know if I can ever make it up to you. I treated you horribly."

"You've already apologized a million times. Enough already."

Everyone made mistakes. *Hers was super sucky, but what can I say? I wasn't perfect.* I blew her a kiss then turned to find where I'd kicked off my shoes in her disaster of a room.

"Aren't you going to do anything to your hair? I can curl it for you if you want. Or straighten it."

"Nah, I like it the way it is." And so did Damon, plus I wouldn't change my appearance for anyone. Stuff like that had never mattered to me before, and it still didn't.

Once I found my heels, I slipped them on and grabbed my black clutch on loan from Mom. It wasn't long before the guys arrived, and we had to deal with a million pictures from our parents before escaping to the dance. Gia and I exchanged a look. It was so weird. I'd never wanted to go to a dance before, but I'd been looking forward to it all week.

On Damon's arm, I entered the gym. One of the two chaperones standing sentry at the threshold placed a pink-and-white-flower crown on my head. I briefly touched the soft petals with the tips of my fingers then sucked in a breath as the full force of the decorated interior hit me.

My step stuttered, and I clung tightly to Damon's solid strength. "It's beautiful."

He tilted his head, a sexy grin curving his mouth. "You're more beautiful, Sky."

I rolled my eyes and tried to ignore the heat that settled into my cheeks as I leaned into him. It looked nothing like the gym. The theme was Enchanted Garden, and the party committee had created pure magic.

Ivy with twinkle lights woven through it climbed the closed bleachers on either side of the gym. Along the edges of the large space were tables set with electric votive candles. Green silk tablecloths fell to the floor, enhancing the outdoor theme. Some tables had petals scattered over the surface, and others had small sprays of wildflowers. Behind the DJ, opposite where we'd entered, hung a backdrop of a darkening sky behind tree silhouettes with the hazy glow of night-lights flittering through them.

There was so much to take in. Lush greenery and cascading blooms hung from the ceiling amid twinkling lights and crystal chandeliers. Tree props with moss and lanterns hung from branches that created gnarled canopies over handfuls of tables.

Damon led me farther into the room, revealing even more surprises. A bench formed from faux driftwood that curled and arched had been tucked into a corner. A fountain with a cascade of lights in place of the water shimmered not far from us. And in the center, a dark-wood pergola decorated with vines and white flowers edged the corners of the dance floor.

Gia and Tucker split off to find his friends somewhere during our walk. I would catch up with her soon, ideally on the dance floor. Damon and I stopped at a table where Phoenix and his date for the night—Lydia—Shane, and Tracey sat. I set my clutch on the table and said hello.

Familiar, upbeat music spilled from the strategically placed speakers. It didn't take long for Damon to take my hand and lead me onto the dance floor, where we lost an hour having more fun than I could remember. I couldn't imagine a night better than this one. I wasn't sure I wanted it to end.

Desperate to slip off my shoes for a little while, I tugged on Damon's arm. "Let's take a break."

He nodded, and we returned to our table. I was overheated but smiled as his cousins and a few football team members chatted with us. Several of my friends also stopped at our table to talk for a few minutes.

Damon was talking to his cousins when I slipped away to get a drink. I stood by the refreshments table, reminiscing over how far I'd come from hating all athletes, the Elite included, to joining in with the rest of the football fans and screaming my head off during the games. The biggest change of all was me dating one of the team's star players.

Strong arms wrapped around my waist and pulled me back against a hard chest. I didn't even need to turn around to know who it was. Those familiar pings of electricity permeated the air around Damon, and my body reacted to his presence.

I turned in his embrace and wrapped my arms around his neck. He grinned, and everything he felt about me, from love to lust, shone in his eyes. I felt safe and so very wanted.

"Have I told you how gorgeous you look?"

"Only about a dozen times." God, I loved everything about him—even his crazy alpha tendencies. "How long do we have to stay here?" I toyed with the ends of his hair.

"You're not enjoying our first official date?" A wicked gleam entered his eyes before he bent and trailed kisses along my neck. When his lips found my ear, he whispered, "I know a place we can go if you want a change of scenery."

That familiar buzz hummed through me, and my nerve endings heightened at the thought of where he wanted to go. "Yeah, I want to go there, but after we dance for a little while."

I wanted the whole experience, and when he pulled back, he must've seen that because he took my hand in his and led me to the dance floor.

The DJ the academy had hired slowed things down, and Damon pulled me back into his arms seconds before the music cut off. Bethany, the student council president, took the stage to announce the homecoming king and queen. I twisted in his arms, leaning back against his chest so I could watch whoever got called up on stage get crowned.

It would be one of the Elite. It always was. And I was good with that. Gia wasn't far, and I flashed her a smile. I couldn't help but wonder if it would be her.

Bethany spoke in her usual on-speed manner. I managed to pick out Damon's name for homecoming king, and the crowd erupted in cheers. He laughed, but I knew he didn't care about any of it. When he made no move to go up, I tried to shove his arms from around my waist so he could claim the crown, but he bent to my ear.

"Wait for it."

"And this year's homecoming queen is our very own blogger extraordinaire, Skylar McCormick!"

Huh, I wasn't sure how I felt about that. I gave him a side-eye when he released me. We went up on stage together, my hand firmly in his much larger one. Several shrill whistles cut through the cheers, and when my gaze fell on Gia and Tucker's wide grins and the other writers in our small editorial group jumping up and down and shouting my name, warmth spread through me. I enjoyed the moment without pretense.

Damon's arm remained around me the entire time, and I leaned into him and smiled. Maybe I didn't mind the spotlight as much as I'd thought. After we were crowned with faux jewels instead of flowers and Damon gave a short speech, we found ourselves back on the dance floor for the "royal" dance.

"Were you responsible for this?" I asked.

His deep laughter rippled over my exposed skin, and I shivered. He had such an effect on me.

"Not really. I mentioned it to a friend who talked to a friend… but you deserve it."

"Thank you." And I meant it. I didn't care if the reason I got on stage with him was less than a hundred percent genuine because it had stemmed from his widespread influence. I had him, and our relationship was real.

"You look pretty amazing with that crown on your head." That same dark, wicked gleam entered his eyes again, and I shivered in anticipation. "It would look much better if you weren't wearing anything." He licked his bottom lip, and my body heated. "Maybe we'll keep the heels."

He bent and kissed me right there on the dance floor, and everything faded to just us. When he pulled back, we both breathed heavily. I wanted him, always. And escaping the dance couldn't happen soon enough. I wanted to be alone with him.

"Thank you for being my date," he said.

The music changed, and the rhythm thumped to the beat of my heart as more people joined us on the dance floor.

"Have you decided on a college yet? I'm signing for Thane in a few days," he added.

"Thane is a good choice."

"Skylar." His growl made me laugh.

"Yes. I'm going there too. How could I not? You'll be there."

"You're what I'm looking forward to during college." He cupped the side of my face and brushed the pad of his thumb over my bottom lip.

"You know that for sure?" I teased because, deep down, I wasn't worried at all. After our somewhat rocky start, he'd set his sights firmly on me, and they hadn't wavered. "A ton of girls there will be thirsty for the new football star joining the team."

"I only need you, but if you want me to prove it to you"—he bent and took my lips in a drugging kiss—"we can go to the basement now, and I'll spend the rest of the night building my case."

I laughed. "I might take you up on that." And not for any other reason than I wanted him just as much.

"Good, because this night is the beginning of the rest of our lives."

He squeezed me tight, and it wasn't long before we slipped away from the other partiers. *Who would've thought a few months ago that my life would have worked out like this?* My mom was safe, and we were both happier than we'd ever thought possible, and the night had already proven magical.

A thrill raced through me because I knew it would be one hell of a future with Damon by my side.

CHAPTER THIRTY-FOUR

DAMON

#Graduation

Graduation had finally arrived, and I was one step closer to college and playing ball with my brother again, and that night, we would have the end-of-high-school bonfire at the beach behind our house. All I had to do was get through the day, then the rest of our lives would begin.

The ceremony was outside, and I'd already taken pictures with my cousins and family. Then more at Sky's house. Her mom, who'd insisted I call her Megan instead of Mrs. McCormick, wanted pictures of us before and after the ceremony.

I waited for Sky to grab her purse and shove in a few last-minute things. My mind wandered to what lay ahead. I had a few weeks before practice started at Thane. Before I left, we planned to have lazy days at the beach, sunning and surfing—or in Sky's case, playing Frisbee.

That would change. All those hours of yoga hadn't just helped me with my agility in football. They would translate to surfing easily, which I planned on teaching her. She just didn't know it yet.

Then, during our winter break, I would take her to see the snow. She'd told me her mom had wanted to take her when they'd planned to make a run for it. A spark of curiosity had lit deep in her clear blue eyes, and I'd vowed to make it happen.

As for the rest of the year, I didn't know where it would lead. I'd had no idea I would end up with a steady girlfriend or a starting position as a running back for Thane—though I'd had a better shot of that than a relationship—and I would continue to fix things with my dad. They weren't back to what they had been, but we were trying.

"Hey." Sky joined me, her graduation gown on a hanger as she shut the door behind her.

I couldn't stop looking at her. It didn't matter what she wore. She was always stunning. She'd chosen a deep-blue maxi skirt that floated around her ankles when she walked, with a form-fitting charcoal-gray sleeveless shirt that ended an inch above her waist, giving me a glimpse of her soft, toned skin.

"We have an hour before we need to be at the ceremony. What do you have planned?"

I laced her fingers with mine and tugged her toward my Range Rover. "Just a short trip to the cove before the craziness of today." After opening her door, I took the hanger from her to put it in the back with mine, then I shut her door.

The twenty-minute drive flew by, and we climbed back out of the SUV. I grinned as her face lit up when she saw the over-sized beach blanket spread out on the small, sandy section.

"When did you do this?" She slipped her arm around my waist and squeezed.

"Early this morning. I wanted to do something together before we got swept away."

She laughed. "Yeah, it's going to be packed with the ceremony, lunch out with all our families, then the beach party tonight."

We would eat with my cousins, Aunt Cece, my dad, Raelyn, Cole, Riley, Megan, and Gia and her parents as well as Tucker and his, since Tucker and Gia were dating. It wouldn't be a quick meal, but I was strangely all right with that, so long as Sky and I had our time together first.

Two water bottles and a vase full of wildflowers waited for us on the blanket. We sat down, and she immediately leaned over to breathe in the scent of the vibrant flowers on her other side. I didn't want any space between us and tugged her closer so I could feel her body pressed against mine.

"They're beautiful, Damon. Thank you." She tilted her head and looked up at me then smiled.

I'd always thought she was gorgeous, but I wanted to give her the world when she looked at me and smiled. "Do you know you're the only girl who has ever turned her nose up at me?"

"And turned you down," she teased, resting her hand on my thigh.

I leaned forward a little, grasped her by the hips, then lifted her so she could straddle me. She adjusted her skirt so it pooled around her, revealing her long, toned legs on either side of mine.

"You made me want you even more," I confessed. "We didn't do anything the traditional way."

Laughter fell from her full lips. "No. I can hardly call black-mailing me for 'favors'"—she air-quoted—"or fake dating as traditional."

I shrugged, enjoying the weight of her hands on my shoulders. "It worked for us."

"Yeah." Her voice softened, and she glanced at my lips then back up. "It did."

"You're incredible. I don't know if I've told you that or not."

She rolled her eyes. "You may have mentioned a time or two that you like how I look."

I grinned. "You're not wrong there, but I meant you're intelligent, funny, adventurous, and very strong. I never thought I would have a girlfriend, and if I had to go back and do things differently, I wouldn't change a thing, because it brought us together, and you're the best thing that's happened to me."

Her eyes widened. "Better than signing with Thane and finding out you'll be a starter?"

I nodded. "Yes. I love you, Sky. More than I ever thought possible."

Her blue eyes misted, and her lower lip trembled. "I love you, too, Damon. And I wouldn't change a thing either."

It was a good thing I'd set an alarm on my phone for when we had to leave. Because when I kissed her, everything faded except the warmth of her body pressed against mine and the softness of her lips. The ever-present connection between us sparked even hotter, and I ran my hand up her thigh, swallowing the sweet sound of her moan.

I would never get enough of her.

When my phone's alarm blasted through the web of desire entangling us, I broke our kiss. Inches separated our lips, and I groaned at the interruption. My hands on her hips, I lifted her with me as I stood until she slid her long legs down my body. When I was sure she was steady, I released her and bent to retrieve our things. She held the flowers as we walked hand in hand to my SUV.

"Are you ready?" I asked.

It was a loaded question, and because it was Sky, she grinned right back. The spark in her eyes told me she understood the hidden message within. It wasn't just about graduation. And when she nodded, my heart swelled with love for her, knowing that was the day our future would begin.

The End

Continue reading the Hidden Valley Elite series with Cruel
Start:
https://www.islavaughnauthor.com/books

Keep up with Isla's releases by joining her newsletter:
https://bit.ly/IslaVaughnNewsletter
If you enjoyed reading Brutal Nights, I hope you'll consider
leaving a review.

ABOUT THE AUTHOR

Isla Vaughn is the author of the Hidden Valley Elite series. Her romance books are full of complex characters, strong alpha males, and the fierce women who bring them to their knees. When not writing, she can be found daydreaming about owning a beach house, reading, or drinking too much coffee.

You can find her at:
https://www.islavaughnauthor.com

Subscribe to Isla's newsletter for cover reveals, book announcements, and giveaways:
https://bit.ly/IslaVaughnNewsletter

instagram.com/islavaughnauthor
goodreads.com/islavaughn_author
tiktok.com/@islavaughnauthor
bookbub.com/profile/isla-vaughn
facebook.com/author.IslaVaughn
twitter.com/IVaughn_Author

ALSO BY ISLA VAUGHN

Hidden Valley Elite Series

Savage Start

Savage Lies

Savage Truth

Brutal Days

Brutal Nights

Cruel Start

Cruel Hate

Cruel Love

Wicked Games

Wicked Ends